How could one kiss change so much?

He was as brain-dead as a lovesick teenager. He was afraid when he saw her again he'd drop to one knee and propose.

It wasn't the first time the notion of remarriage had crossed his mind, but it *was* the first time he'd put a face to that vague image of the woman who'd fit the mold he had made for himself.

Callie Brockman.

What was so crazy about his thoughts was that she wasn't the type of woman he'd considered marriage material at all.

Callie was nothing less than a gun-toting spitfire who turned his insides to mush.

Books by Deb Kastner

Love Inspired

A Holiday Prayer #46
Daddy's Home #55
Black Hills Bride #90
The Forgiving Heart #113

DEB KASTNER

Deb is the wife of a Reformed Episcopal minister, so it was natural for her to find her niche in the Christian/inspirational romance market. She enjoys tackling the issues of faith and trust within the context of a romance. Her characters range from upbeat and humorous to (her favorite) dark and brooding heroes. Her plots fall anywhere between, from a playful romp to the deeply emotional.

When she's not writing, she enjoys spending time with her husband and three girls and, whenever she can manage, attending regional dinner theater and touring Broadway musicals.

The Forgiving Heart
Deb Kastner

Love Inspired®

Published by Steeple Hill Books™

STEEPLE HILL BOOKS

Steeple
Hill™

ISBN 0-373-87119-8

THE FORGIVING HEART

Visit us at www.steeplehill.com

Printed in U.S.A.

"I was in prison and you came to Me." Then the righteous will answer Him, saying, "Lord, when did we see You...in prison, and come to You?" And the King will answer and say to them, "Assuredly, I say to you, inasmuch as you did it to one of the least of these, my brethren, you did it to Me."

—*Matthew* 25:36-40

To my sister Amy.

I'm blessed to be your relative,
but so much more to be your friend.

Keep chasing the wind,
and don't ever let anyone talk you out of it!

Chapter One

The young man set his jaw, his throat corded with strain. Surprisingly dark eyebrows scrunched grimly over wide blue eyes, a shady contrast to his closely cropped golden-blond hair. Long, muscular arms with hands tightly fisted crossed over a chest just beginning to show a hint of breadth.

He looked angry. Resentful. Bitter.

Scared completely out of his wits.

Officer Callie Brockman felt an unfamiliar wave of emotion she could only classify as maternal instinct, however misplaced and foreign.

She quickly masked it with her usual armor, her way of getting by in the world. Anger.

Fortunately, even that was easily hidden. Callie

Brockman was an expert in concealing her true feelings. She'd learned early that it was best to reveal as little as possible about what she was thinking and feeling. Life was safer that way.

"What's the kid in for?" she asked Bobby, the middle-aged dispatcher sporting a paunch and a bald spot. She nodded toward the benched teenager, who had unfolded his arms and was clenching his hands together and glaring a hole in the floor.

Who, she wondered, could leave a youth to fend for himself like this, though her acrimony didn't show in her tone. Unfortunately, she had a pretty good guess about the boy's parents, or lack of them. She just hadn't expected to deal with this so soon.

Not in such a small town. Why had she moved to John Day, Oregon, if not to slow down and find a more deliberate way of life?

Bobby stretched back in his oversize office chair and ruffled the short, spiked ends of his black hair—what was left of it, anyway—with the tips of his fingers.

"Shoplifting. Classic case."

"Yeah?" As the newest police officer on the force, it was her job to take on the juvies. She shook her head in reluctant acceptance of this part of her job. It was unavoidable, she knew, but still…

This was only her second night on the job, and already, a *classic* case to handle. She sighed under her breath.

Couldn't she have gone for at least a week without a *classic* case? She'd hoped for better in a small town, having come from fast-paced, crime-ridden Portland where juvenile crime was at an all-time high.

But this wasn't Portland. Everyone knew everyone in John Day, most from several generations. More than likely, she'd met this kid's parents already; if not at the post office, then perhaps in line at the grocery store or the local deli.

If somehow she'd missed out on meeting them already, though, the slight was about to be remedied, and not in pleasant circumstances, either. It wasn't a thought she wished to dwell on, so she turned to the paperwork Bobby shoved at her.

She ran down the teen's file in short order. There wasn't much to see.

Brandon Wheeler. Sixteen. First time offender.

Wheeler. The name sounded familiar, though she couldn't immediately place it.

"Oh, man," said Bobby, whistling under his breath. "His old man's going to pitch a fit when he finds out about this.'' He punctuated his sentence with a negative grunt.

"Wheeler?" she asked, hoping he'd clue her in. The more she knew about this kid's parents, the easier processing the criminal would go. And as far as Callie was concerned, the easier, the better. She wasn't big on tough cases.

"Everett Wheeler. Goes by Rhett. Community service agent," Bobby supplied.

Rhett Wheeler. *That's* where she'd heard the name before. The kid in question was the son of the community service agent.

It figured. It just figured.

Bad luck followed her around like a little black rain cloud hovering directly over her head. She'd hoped changing locales would help her lose the shady veil, but obviously she'd been mistaken.

A woman couldn't run from herself.

Her gaze returned to the young man slouching on the bench, looking increasingly miserable with every tick of the clock. She could only imagine what had gone through that boy's mind, what would prompt a handsome kid like Brandon Wheeler to break the law.

Actually, she *could* imagine why a seemingly typical teen would commit a crime. She remembered all too well.

She blew out a breath and turned away, unwilling to revive memories she thought had been laid to rest.

It hurt to be a cop and have to face these kids and their parents. The pain of it scratched black marks in her heart. She'd run away from it if she was able, but that was beyond her capabilities.

Whatever internal wounds she incurred as a police officer, it hurt far more to stand around and do nothing.

With effort, she reined in the empathetic sting of bitterness she felt at seeing Brandon Wheeler shuddering in his tennis shoes.

She was a cop. A juvenile cop, at the moment. And she had work to do, however distasteful.

"He's been booked and fingerprinted," Bobby said, answering her unspoken question. "You can call his dad to pick him up, or you can take him home yourself, if you'd like."

Her gaze snapped up in surprise. "Take him home?"

Bobby chuckled and patted his ample midsection. "Sure. There's not a whole lot else going on here tonight, in case you hadn't noticed."

Callie pressed her lips together, leaving her thoughts unspoken. *Portland* police didn't escort their young criminals home. Many young people stayed in jail overnight—or sometimes even longer—when uncaring or absent parents didn't respond.

Who was she to say this small-town police department was making a mistake? Maybe they were right, giving a little personality to their police department. Especially for the kids' sake.

She paced toward Brandon Wheeler until she stood directly in front of him. He avoided her eyes, glaring unseeingly at a point near his knees.

"You want me to give you a lift? Or should I call your mom to come get you?"

"No!" The towheaded youth came alive, bounding to his feet. "I mean, yes, ma'am."

He reached for her arm, then appeared to realize what he was doing and dropped his hand, stuffing it in the pocket of his blue jeans. He looked up at her, and then down at the floor again, toeing the tile with the tip of his sneaker. "I—I guess I'd…" He paused, continuing to toe the tile. "I'd rather have you drive me home."

He shrugged as if he didn't care one way or the other. "If you don't mind." And then as an afterthought, he added, "Ma'am."

Ma'am? Her eyes narrowed speculatively on the boy. This was certainly the first time she'd been called *ma'am* by a juvenile delinquent, at least without prodding.

This kid was too polite by far, setting off warning bells in Callie's head, which she studiously ignored.

Brandon Wheeler wasn't any of her business.

"First offense?" she barked at Brandon, though of course she already knew the answer. She'd worked with hundreds of teenage offenders in Portland, kids no different from Brandon except they'd been born on the wrong side of the tracks in a city that didn't give second chances.

This kid was probably nothing more than the small-town version of the big-city type. Same song, different verse.

She gestured the youth ahead of her, then studied him on the way out to her patrol car. Brandon Wheeler was too soft for crime.

Real crime, anyway.

He was clean-cut. A mom-country-and-apple-pie kind of small-town kid, the brand of youth Uncle Sam dreamed about. Unfortunately, she already knew the tune this kid was playing. She'd heard it before, and not just from her work as a police officer. It hit too close for comfort. *Way* too close.

Seeing Brandon safely into the netted back seat

of the car, she slid in behind the steering wheel and turned the key in the ignition. It was a mere three-minute drive to the address Brandon provided. Not much time to chat.

Besides, the youth was still surly, though he was reluctantly cooperative to the few requests she'd made of him.

She glanced in the rearview mirror, taking further assessment of her charge. One thing was certain—he was going to end up with a killer headache if he kept gritting his teeth.

It occurred to Callie to provoke him into speech, but he looked as if he might cry, though she knew he'd deny it vehemently if she voiced her concern.

Give this kid a break, she prayed silently, awkwardly. She and God weren't exactly on a first-name basis, but this seemed as good a time as any to make an exception.

She'd do just about anything to keep from having a crying kid on her hands, especially one that was tugging at her heartstrings.

She was a little frightened she might cry, too. For whatever reason, her carefully maintained dam of emotions appeared to have been compromised.

She wondered if she ought to attempt to strike

up a conversation with Brandon, to take his mind off his trouble, if that was possible. At any rate, *she* could stand to think about something besides the unfortunate first meeting to come, with the social worker who'd be taking her caseloads.

Brandon's father.

She'd be working closely with Rhett Wheeler, and the very first time they were introduced, it had to be when she was bringing his own kid home to him from the police station on a shoplifting indictment.

Maybe she'd get lucky and Rhett wouldn't be home. Maybe she'd be able to put off the inevitable, at least for the moment.

Yeah, and maybe pigs would fly.

"Hang in there, kid."

The moment the words left her mouth, she wanted to bang her forehead against the steering wheel. How idiotic could she be? In her experience, teenage boys did *not* like to be called *kid,* and she'd just flunked Juvenile Cop 101.

Brandon, who'd been staring grimly out the window, whipped his head around front, the whites of his eyes gleaming in the reflection of passing street lamps.

Callie held her breath, waiting for him to tell her what he *really* thought of this situation.

He cleared his throat, licked his lips and uttered a single word. "Thanks."

What?

Surprise jolted through her, which was no doubt the instigator of her next words, which were every bit as idiotic as her first.

"You want to talk about it?"

"No."

Short, sweet and to the point. She chuckled. "I figured."

The boy grunted.

She glanced in the rearview mirror, catching his wide-eyed gaze, which reminded her of a deer caught in headlights. Again, Callie found herself feeling for Brandon, wondering why he'd committed a crime.

"Just one question."

"Do I need a lawyer?"

The kid cracked a joke under pressure. Callie grinned despite herself. She liked him more and more by the minute. Too bad there were only a few minutes left between them.

"This is strictly off the record."

"Yeah?"

"Yeah."

To her surprise, he smiled, making his face turn

from surly to downright cute. He'd be a knockout when he grew into his shoulders.

"What's a kid like me doing in a place like this?" he quipped.

Astounded, she laughed out loud. "I'll admit the question crossed my mind once or twice." A hundred times, she amended silently.

A kid like Brandon didn't just put a department store T-shirt on over his own and waltz out in direct view of everyone unless he had good reason. Even rookie shoplifters had more sense than that.

Especially rookie shoplifters.

Which could only mean Brandon had another reason for breaking the law, and Callie's guess was that he was doing it to get attention—most likely his parents' attention.

Anger flared a familiar fire in her chest, but she tamped it back. It really wasn't any of her business. Not beyond doing her civic duty.

She'd drop Brandon off, go home to her tiny cottage and spend the night screaming into her pillow if that's what it took.

What she would *not* do—could not do—is crack the facade she'd taken so long to acquire.

Pulling onto Brandon's street, she parked in the

driveway he indicated and shut down the motor. She took two deep breaths before speaking.

"You ready?"

She wasn't.

He shrugged, his eyebrows a grim line again. "Guess so."

"Think your dad is home?" she asked, holding her breath for the answer.

She *really* didn't want to know. She *really* didn't want to do this.

"Yeah. The light is on."

"Couldn't that be your mother?"

His jaw clenched as he swallowed hard. "She checked out when I was eight."

"Checked out?" replied Callie, scrambling to backtrack, feeling as if she'd taken the first step off a dangerously high cliff.

Checked out. The words made her shiver.

"Left. You know. Took off. To find herself, or whatever."

She felt it when he punched the back of the front seat, but she didn't draw attention to the fact. She'd punch something, too, if she could.

"She didn't come back. Dad said it was because of her health, but…" He slammed his jaw shut as if he'd said too much already.

"I'm sorry," she murmured, not knowing what else to say.

And she *was* sorry. Brandon's revelation explained, in part, anyway, what was bothering him.

Losing a mother was a traumatic experience, especially if she abandoned her family first.

What kind of a mother left an eight-year-old kid on his own and didn't look back? Callie reminded herself there were two sides to every story, but she couldn't help but toss her own judgment into the ring.

Brandon just shrugged, his eyebrows making a dark V over his nose. "No big deal. She died a little while after that, so I guess it didn't matter much either way."

She cringed inside, wishing she had some words of wisdom that would make Brandon feel better. But what could she say? How could she express her sympathy to a boy she barely knew?

Taking a deep, calming breath, she released Brandon from the back seat and gestured for him to precede her to the porch. Her mind spun with questions.

Why would Brandon break the law? And why now, and not last year, or next year? It wasn't as if his grief over his mother were fresh fodder. It had been years since she died.

Years for resentment and bitterness to grow and fester. Years for Brandon's self-esteem to wither to the point where he'd try to get his deficit father's attention by shoplifting.

The youth seemed bright enough on the outside, but he was obviously hiding a great, deep hurt—something he couldn't settle on his own.

How, she wondered, did Rhett Wheeler fit into this near-violent turbulence? Had he run Brandon's mother off? Was he an absentee father? Cold? Abusive?

Reluctantly, she raised her hand to the door and knocked. Her stomach quivered as a chill washed over her.

She had the strangest feeling she was going to find out exactly what was wrong, why Brandon had acted the way he had and how Rhett Wheeler fit into this picture.

She was an unwilling victim. Truth be told, she didn't really want to know.

Chapter Two

Brandon!

At the firm knock on the front door, Rhett bolted out of his leather easy chair, and blitzed toward the entry, his slippers scuffing lightly on the carpet.

Brandon had a key. Why wasn't he using it?

Rhett didn't have to look at his watch to know his son was four hours late getting home from school, even if he'd stayed to play a game of football with his friends.

And he didn't have to look too deeply into his heart to know why.

Guilt edged through him. They hadn't been getting along very well lately. He and Brandon hadn't been getting along at *all*. He had no idea what had gotten into his teenage son—or maybe it was just a stage teens went through.

How was he supposed to know what to do with a boy who thought he knew everything and disagreed with everything Rhett said?

If he said the sky was blue, by golly, Brandon thought it was yellow, and said so quite adamantly. If Rhett threw on a classical CD, Brandon countered it with a loud, thumping bass that made Rhett's head ache just thinking about it.

And he was thinking about it.

He'd been sitting in the den in the half dark, with only the desk lamp on low, wondering where things had gone wrong. More to the point, how could he fix it?

What had happened to the closeness he'd shared with his son as a child? Now, he might as well be speaking a different language, for all Brandon listened to him. Rhett was stunned by the change.

Maybe if Kayla was still alive he wouldn't be having all these problems with Brandon. The poor kid hadn't had the benefit of a mother's influence during the rocky teenage years.

No.

What good did it do to wish for something that

couldn't be? Where was his faith? Hadn't God placed him in this situation? He wasn't the world's first single father, and he wouldn't be the last. Or the worst. Of that, he was certain.

"What did you do, forget your—" Rhett's words slammed to a halt in his throat as he encountered the glint of a police badge reflected off the porch light, and then caught up in his breath when he looked at the serious, silver-blue eyes of the woman wearing the uniform.

As the community counselor and social worker, he knew every officer on the police force. But he *sure* hadn't seen this lady around.

He might be an early widower, but he wasn't blind.

She was tall, five-eight or five-nine, he guessed, with short blond hair that glistened in the moonlight. She was slim, with womanly curves in all the right places despite the ill-fitting polyester uniform.

Her classic profile created quite an entrancing silhouette, what with her high cheekbones and a long, straight nose.

All this he appreciated, as only a man can appreciate a woman. But what drew him most, what made him do a double take inside and out, was the sparkle in her eyes.

She noticed him notice her and lifted one frosty eyebrow, her lightly glossed lips pressed in a firm, straight line.

Flustered, his gaze slid to the right of the policewoman and landed squarely on his son. At the same moment Rhett realized the urgent nature of the situation, Brandon tipped his chin defiantly in the air, though he didn't quite meet his father's now serious gaze.

"What...?" Rhett croaked, his stomach cinching tight. He didn't know what was going on, but it wasn't good, not with the way Brandon clenched and unclenched his fists, looking like he wanted to dig his way to China if given half the chance.

The cop pierced him with a thinly masked glare, and he took two mental steps backward. She sized him up in detail before answering his half-question, her gaze probing his.

Uncomfortable with the intensity of her scrutiny, he swallowed hard and slid his gaze back to his son, who had neither moved nor spoken in the interim.

"Mr. Wheeler," the flashy lady cop began, her voice, soft and silver-toned, belying her tight expression. "I'm afraid your son has visited us at the precinct. He's been caught..."

She paused and pinched her lips even more tightly together, looking decidedly uncomfortable, as if her thick polyester uniform had suddenly become too tight.

"What?" he demanded, his voice low and coarse.

"Um…" she shrugged "—shoplifting."

She'd said the word so softly it was as if she hadn't wanted him to hear. But he'd heard. Loud and clear.

"Brandon *stole* something?" he roared, narrowing his furious gaze on his son, who shifted from one foot to the other and looked at the ground.

He shifted his gaze back to the officer, demanding an explanation with his expression if not his words. Her eyes sparkled with what he thought might be amusement, which only served to up his emotional ante.

"That's the generally accepted definition of *shoplifting*."

Rhett's blood went from hot to boiling, pounding through his veins. His temper fared no better, and her idea of a joke did nothing to alleviate his fury. If she thought this was funny…

"Brandon Adam," he bellowed, grabbing his

son by the collar of his coat, "Get your sorry
carcass in this house *now*."

Brandon tensed and pulled against his grasp,
the boy's gaze darting to the left and right as if
he were considering making a mad dash down the
darkened street. Rhett was good and ready to follow him.

One more look at his father clenched the matter, as Brandon appeared to think better of it, and
slipped quickly past Rhett and into the house, running as soon as he made it through the door.

Rhett listened to the pounding of Brandon's
footsteps on the stairs leading up to his bedroom,
but didn't relax until he heard the door to the
boy's room slam closed.

Brandon would stay put, if he knew what was
good for him. He was in a heap of trouble, and
he had a world of explaining to do.

Rhett felt a light grip on his forearm, and
looked down to see the officer's hand resting on
his bare skin, which prickled as if touched by an
electrical current under her gentle touch.

He stepped back, as outraged by the fact that
he noticed—no, *responded*—to the attractive lady
police officer holding on to his arm, as he was
that she was still standing on his porch in the first
place.

She'd obviously stuck around to watch him bluster through this whole pathetic attempt at fatherhood, and a sorry attempt it was.

Was she judging him on what she saw?

Her next words confirmed the worst. "Go easy on the boy, Rhett. It's his first offense."

Her tone was soft. Kind. Filled with genuine concern.

And completely out of line. He didn't want, or *need*, her suggestions or her interference.

Does the word privacy *mean anything to you?* He bit the inside of his lip to keep from saying the words aloud.

"Look Ms.—" he paused, his gaze sliding to her name plate "—Brockman."

"Callie," she correctly softly, in a voice that would have otherwise engaged him.

"Whatever."

He blew out a breath and jammed his fingers into his thick, light-brown hair. He wore it a good inch longer than the typical businessman's, an inch and a half over the buzz-cut cops he worked with. He might not be in fashion, but then, Rhett rarely was. Nor did he care.

"Look, I appreciate your bringing Brandon home and all. Thank you for the extra effort. However—"

She cut him off midsentence—before he'd attempted to get her out of here. He wanted to be upstairs with his son, but courtesy dictated he get rid of Ms. Brockman first. And fast, hopefully.

"It was no trouble," she said, flashing him a quick, bright smile. "I was glad to do it."

"Again, Ms. Bro—uh, Callie. Thank you."

Anyone else would have recognized his words as the dismissal they were, Rhett thought, incensed, but Officer Callie Brockman was either uncommonly imperceptive or acutely stubborn. Looking into her fixed gaze, Rhett was inclined to believe the latter.

"It's his first offense," Callie repeated, her voice at once intense and uncertain.

"You don't have to tell me that," Rhett snapped. It wasn't as if he hadn't heard her the first time. *Or* that he wasn't aware of his own son's lack of a criminal record—at least until tonight.

Still, he gave her the benefit of the doubt. She could legitimately be trying to be helpful.

Nevertheless, Rhett wanted her gone. Now.

Softening his voice, he continued. "I know he'll be facing a court date and all, but I'd appreciate it if we could discuss Brandon's situation some other time. Right now, I have a son to rake over the coals. Hot coals.''

It was the wrong thing to say. He knew it—and regretted it—the moment the words passed his lips, especially when Callie took a quick step backward and inhaled sharply, as if she'd been struck.

Exasperation quickly replaced any guilt he might have harbored had she not glared daggers at him. It wasn't as if he were going to take a stick to Brandon, though heaven knew the boy deserved whatever he got.

He was a social worker, for pity's sake, not to mention a Christian. He knew the rules of the state—and the love of God.

There was one other thing he knew for certain. What he did or did not do to—or with—his son *sure* wasn't any of *her* business.

"Good night, Officer Brockman." This time, he purposefully chose the formal use of her name, in case she was a little slow taking a hint. Which, of course, she appeared to be.

Determined to put an abrupt end to any further arguments she might pose, he stepped backward and swung the door closed.

To his surprise, it bounced back open a few inches from the doorjamb.

With an audible sigh, he looked down through his dark scowl to find a dainty foot, albeit clad in county-issued dress-black shoes, blocking the door's natural progress.

Silver-blue eyes glared at him through the crack made by her foot, and then she moved closer, stabbing him with her now one-eyed gaze. All he could see besides the eye was one scrunched blond eyebrow and half a frown.

What was he supposed to do now?

Several distinctly un-Christian thoughts crossed his mind. But in the end, he groaned and stepped back, allowing the door to swing open another foot—*exactly* one foot. That was *all* he was going to give.

"Are you going to listen to me or not?" she demanded, her voice a high squeak.

It occurred to him he might find humor in the situation at a later occasion, once he cooled off. Come to think of it, this whole night would make a good story to tell around the family campfire years from now.

But at the moment, he was as mad as a hornet ready for the sting. Angry at Callie, at Brandon, and most of all, at himself.

Somehow, it always boiled down to *him* in the end.

"Well?" she asked, sounding not only annoyed, but impatient.

"What choice do you leave me?" he muttered irritably under his breath.

She caught his sarcasm anyway, and even had an answer. "None whatsoever."

He mentally nixed *uncommonly imperceptive* and ran the flag up for *acutely stubborn*. Callie Brockman was quite possibly the most stubborn woman he'd ever had the *dis*pleasure of meeting.

And he a social worker and psychologist. A people person. Was he simply missing the point?

Callie obviously thought so.

He frowned and tried to think about the situation from her perspective. She was a cop, and new in town, to boot. Didn't lady cops have to be bad to the bone to survive against their peers? Not to mention the criminal element.

He'd give her one more tiny chance to redeem herself, he decided quickly. Maybe she had something worthwhile to say behind all that bluff and blunder.

"Make it quick," he growled, continuing to hold the door open exactly one foot and not an inch more.

"Your *son* put a department store T-shirt on *over* his own shirt with the plastic surveillance tag not only still attached, but in plain sight. He walked right out the front door.''

Rhett's heart dropped like a stone into the pit of his stomach—that is, if he had any heart left at all after her callous pronouncement.

What was this, some kind of teenage prank or double dare? Gang initiation?

But this was *Brandon* they were talking about. His own son, his flesh and blood.

And Rhett *knew* better.

Still, he couldn't help but blurt the question aloud, almost as if Officer Brockman weren't still standing on his doorstep staring him down. "Get to the point. What are you trying to imply?"

She frowned and looked him up and down. "You're a smart man. You figure it out."

She jerked her foot out of the threshold so suddenly that Rhett's weight, as he leaned against the door, had the effect of literally slamming in his own face.

Fury tore through him as he ripped the door back open, heaving it back until it banged against the wall.

"This is none of your business!" he yelled at the receding figure, only afterward realizing the interesting scene he was creating in the neighborhood for the eyes and ears of all his friends and neighbors.

Even then, he couldn't stop himself from having the last word. "You don't know anything about Brandon! *I'm* his father."

Callie froze halfway down the walkway and visibly tensed, but she didn't turn around.

"You want to be a father?" Her words were barely more than a whisper, and filled with so much agony Rhett immediately regretted his unkind words and actions, the way he'd blown her over like a mortar shell.

He was halfway down the walk, preparing to make things right and apologize for his previous words and actions, when she spoke again, bringing him up short.

"A father isn't born." Her silvery voice had transformed into cold steel, matching the crispness of the evening air. "He's made. Do Brandon a favor and act like a *real* father."

Chapter Three

Rhett leaned his forearm on the back of the closed door and blew out a breath. He'd been standing motionless for at least ten minutes, his gaze locked frozenly on the doorknob. Anger, frustration and resentment warred within his chest, causing an almost physical pain.

He slammed the flat of his hand against the back of the door. He didn't make a fist only because he didn't want to have to replace his door.

With an audible huff of breath, he spun around and started up the stairs. He'd made a complete mess of the incident. From start to finish, and every minute in between.

In what was definitely among the most memorable moments of the evening, he'd killed the messenger. Not a pretty sight.

It was bad enough he couldn't reach his own son with God's love, not to mention his own. But to take it out on an innocent bystander—God forgive him.

He slumped against the door frame of his son's room, deflated. Yelling at innocent bystanders wasn't his style, and it certainly wasn't God's style.

As if that weren't enough, he'd actually been attracted to the woman inside the uniform, something that not only surprised him, but threw him for a loop.

Uniforms were supposed to do something to a man's image, but in his experience, uniforms didn't usually do much for the ladies in the force.

At least until tonight.

He had a suspicion Callie Brockman would look good in a gunnysack.

But he wasn't about to go there. Besides, as he'd so succinctly pointed out to Callie earlier, he had a kid to rake over the coals. He wasn't looking forward to it, but he'd put off the inevitable long enough.

He straightened, his fist paused, ready to knock. Yet he hesitated.

He hadn't the slightest idea what to say. Until this moment, Brandon had been the epitome of the ideal student—a player on the varsity football team, popular with the girls and grades good enough for the Ivy League, not that Rhett could afford Ivy anything on his fast-food budget.

How could something like this have happened in John Day? What was the point of living in a small town if it wasn't to avoid bad influences on his kid?

He'd moved here hoping for a new start. How foolish. Trouble followed him like stickpins to a magnet. All he'd done was change the background scenery.

He'd have to talk to Brandon sooner or later, and sooner was probably preferable to later. He knocked crisply, but received no reply.

Consciously controlling his anger, he knocked again, but when the room continued to be silent, he barked out Brandon's name and let himself in.

Brandon was sprawled on his bed, ostensibly engrossed in a sports magazine, though Rhett could tell his attention was elsewhere.

"Brandon Adam," he began in his sternest voice. "We need to talk. Now."

Brandon rolled away from Rhett and tucked one arm under his head, continuing to stare at the slickly glossed magazine and hum to the tense beat of the music on his stereo.

Rhett's mind was whirling, trying to solve the riddle of how to approach his son, who was obviously not going to cooperate. His music only added to the pounding in Rhett's head.

Personally, he was inclined to let the incident slide with just a stiff lecture and a warning not to do it again.

Not only was it Brandon's first offense, but it was clearly done with the intention of getting caught, if Callie's assertions were correct.

"C'mon, kiddo, let's talk this out," he said, amazed at how calm his voice sounded, at odds with the furious pounding of his heart in his head. Until this moment, he'd never realized how difficult parenting could be, and he prayed desperately for the right words to say.

Pray. That was a good idea. "Do you want to pray about it?"

"Don't call me kiddo," Brandon snapped.

"Excuse me?" Rhett barked back, despite his best intentions. "I don't believe I heard you correctly, young man."

"Not like *that's* anything new."

"What?" Rhett was practically screaming now, at least on the inside. His voice was low and cold on the outside. Proverbial steam poured from his ears, and all his good intentions with it. Raw anger sprinted through him, and for a moment he lost his capacity to speak.

"Just leave me alone." Brandon's words met Rhett like a bombshell, and rejection exploded through him. Those were the words Brandon's mother, Kayla, had said to him just before she left him.

Brandon wanted to be alone?

Fine. Rhett could concede to that.

"You're grounded for a month, kiddo," he growled between clenched teeth.

Brandon just grunted in response.

"That means," he continued, pacing the room, "you are to be home directly after school is out for the day. I'll be checking on you at three-fifteen, and you'd better be here. In your room, doing your homework. No exceptions."

"I've got football practice."

"No. You don't." Rhett caught his breath, realizing only after the words were out of his mouth what he had said.

Brandon rolled to his feet, his red face a stark contrast to his white-blond hair. "You can't do this to me!"

In for a penny, in for a pound, Rhett quoted to

himself with an inward sigh. What was done, was done. He couldn't very well back off now.

"Yes, I can. And I have. Do we understand each other?"

Brandon didn't answer.

"Do we understand each other?" Rhett asked again, enunciating every syllable.

"No way. No way are you going to ruin my life," Brandon screamed. "If I don't go out for varsity football this year, there's no way I'll make the starting squad in my senior year."

He pounded his fist into his open palm, but Rhett didn't budge through the outburst.

"It's my only chance to get into a decent college on a football scholarship." Somewhere along the way, his son's tone had turned to pleading.

Which made what had to be done every bit more difficult for Rhett. He clenched his jaw and shook his head. "You have your grades. That'll have to be good enough."

Brandon snorted. "You *know* this is my only chance. You *know* it!"

He threw the magazine at Rhett, who ducked around it, clamping his jaw shut to keep from reneging, or worse yet, reacting to his son's anger in kind.

"You better watch it, mister, or you'll find

yourself packed off to a military boarding school. Serve you right for throwing things at me. Maybe military training will teach you some respect.''

"I hate you. I *hate* you.'' Tears poured down Brandon's cheeks as he tore from the room, slamming the door behind him.

With a tired sigh, Rhett slumped onto Brandon's bed, holding his suddenly aching head in his hands. The pounding had turned to a dull, throbbing ache. "I've really done it this time, God,'' he prayed aloud. "How on earth am I going to get out of this one?''

Chapter Four

Callie hadn't darkened the door of a church in years—not since Colin had been sent away to military school when they were both sixteen. Churches made her nervous, and she wasn't sure she should be here now.

Which explained why she was still in her SUV and not in the chapel. She gripped the steering wheel tightly with both fists and pushed her weight back into the bucket seat until her forearms ached from the tension.

Going to church shouldn't be a big deal. But it was. At least for her.

Her mind flashed back to when she and Colin were seven, and they'd given their hearts to Jesus during vacation Bible school. How simple faith in God had seemed back then.

But that was then. When God took Colin away from her for good, she couldn't bear the thought of going to church without him.

Like most fraternal twins, Callie and Colin had bonded in a special way. Even now there were times when she felt saddened for no apparent reason, or elated or frightened.

It was her only link to Colin, and she treasured those moments, knowing in her heart her twin was alive and well somewhere in the world. Only God knew where.

And He wasn't sharing His knowledge with her. Then again, she wasn't asking for His help.

She didn't know who she was angriest with— God, Colin or her father, for running Colin off in the first place. If only...

But there was no *if only.* She hadn't stood up to Father then, and Colin had disappeared. One youthful prank, and Father had packed Colin off to boarding school.

For his own good.

Even now, her father's dismal words echoed in the recesses of her mind. That memory haunted her to this day, though Father died years ago.

She shook her head. She couldn't imagine

Colin in uniform. He'd been kind and sensitive.
Full of laughter and spontaneity. Not someone
who could handle the tough, impersonal world of
the military.

But Father hadn't seen that. He hadn't cared.
Sending Colin away was probably the easiest
thing he'd ever done.

And when he refused to attend Colin's graduation, and wouldn't even allow her to go...

She should have bucked her father's authority
and gone to see her brother as her heart had
begged for her to do. Maybe if she had, Colin
wouldn't have run off without letting his family
know where he was going.

For eleven long years a part of her heart and
soul was missing. Would she ever feel whole
again?

She doubted it. She really, truly doubted it.

Chimes pealed from the belfry, announcing to
one and all the service at St. James Community
Church was about to start.

Callie blew out a breath and called in every last
bit of her courage. She'd come here to apologize
to Everett Wheeler, and she wasn't leaving until
she'd accomplished that task.

It hadn't taken much prompting for Bobby to
tell her where to find Rhett on a Sunday morning.

Apparently he and Brandon faithfully attended the small church.

It was worth her having to sit through a church service if it meant the opportunity to talk to Rhett. And that's what she was here to do.

He was going to get his apology *today.*

The last thing Callie needed in her new life in John Day was to start off on the wrong foot with the admittedly handsome community service agent. Becoming the leading lady in the *Taming of the Shrew* wasn't exactly what she had in mind.

Bolstering her determination, she locked her car and walked toward the nearest door, head held high and shoulders squared. Her police academy training was holding up in good stead at the moment. No one looking at her would guess she was quaking in her shoes at the thought of entering God's house.

She realized belatedly that the door she'd approached didn't appear to be the main entrance, and she wondered briefly if she ought to walk the perimeter of the church building to look for something more accessible.

"Six of one, half-dozen of the other," she quipped to herself, trying the handle on the door in front of her. If she couldn't find the sanctuary on the first try, at least she might find someone to point her in the right direction.

The handle gave way easily under her touch, and she stepped into a large, echoing, wood-floored room. It was immediately obvious she'd found the gym, and not the sanctuary. Still, she'd gained access, and the sanctuary couldn't be far away.

She was halfway to the hall door when a peculiar thumping sound caught her ear. Her police training took over, and she moved in to investigate.

In the far corner of the room, a boxer's punching bag swayed in the rapid, methodic rhythm of the pounding noise. Someone was obviously trying to work off a bad mood.

Maybe she should invest in a punching bag, given her recent history. The corner of her mouth quivered into a half smile.

Squinting toward the swaying bag, she hesitated, caught between her natural curiosity and desire to help, and the hard-earned knowledge that help was rarely desired or asked for. People liked their privacy, and guarded it jealously. She might be—probably already was—intruding on someone's personal moment.

She was on the verge of leaving for the second

time when an off-center punch threw the bag to the side, and she caught an eyeful of the young man behind the series of angry strokes.

Brandon Wheeler.

Her skin prickled with nervous energy even as her body switched into confrontational mode. Her gaze darted around the room, looking for the striking green eyes of Brandon's father.

Thankfully, he wasn't around. She let out a sigh that was half relief and half annoyance that she'd mustered her defenses for no good reason.

At least she knew Rhett was around someplace, probably worshipping in the sanctuary, joining in song with the others. She should be finding the sanctuary, as well, if the organ music in the background was any indication.

But she needed a minute to compose herself against the emotional roller-coaster ride that got her here in the first place. The congregation joined their voices in a sweet, familiar hymn of praise.

Rhett would be there, his honey-coated tenor blending into the heavenly meter. That thought was almost enough to coax her into joining the service. Was she being sacrilegious to think that way?

Probably. Mentally ducking bolts of lightning, she consciously switched her gaze to Brandon. It couldn't hurt her position any to patch things over with the kid.

"Hey, Brandon," she called in a loud voice, wanting to give fair warning before she approached. Her voice sounded low and scratchy in the echo of the gym. A byproduct of her dry throat, no doubt.

Brandon didn't appear to hear her. Either that or he was purposely ignoring her. He didn't miss a punch, and appeared singularly devoted to mutilating the punching bag in front of him. Sweat dripped off his chin and onto his neatly ironed button-down white oxford shirt.

A sixteen-year-old kid who knew how to iron? Now *there* was a contradiction in terms if she'd ever heard one. She grinned.

"I think it's dead," she offered, slowing the punching bag with the flat of her hand.

Brandon didn't look amused. Startled, maybe, and a little scared. But definitely not amused.

"Hi," she said, focusing on keeping her grin steady. He didn't have to know she was shaky on the inside despite her brave exterior.

"Hi," he responded, his voice squeaking up an octave halfway through the syllable, a most revealing trait in an adolescent boy.

"Remember me? Callie Brockman."

"*Officer* Brockman."

She shrugged, not missing the emphasis on his words. "The one and only."

Did she imagine it, or did the corner of his mouth creep the tiniest bit upward? Suddenly, it felt very important to make the boy smile.

She threw a playful punch at the bag.

"Ouch!" The punching bag was harder than it looked, yet Brandon had been swinging at it barehanded.

She shook her hand out, then assessed it for bruises. "Nothing broken, at least."

She noticed Brandon's knuckles were scraped and bloody, but she continued the one-sided conversation without making mention of his wounds.

"What's in this thing, rocks?"

This time when she hit the bag, she was prepared for the impact.

At long last, Brandon smiled. The rivulets of sweat—possibly, Callie suspected, mixed with tears—poured down his cheeks, sweeping around his mouth and tunneling through the cleft in his chin that was remarkably similar to Rhett's.

Now that she'd had the opportunity to study him in the daylight, she realized just how much he really did look like his father, except that Rhett's hair had darkened with age. She'd bet a month's paycheck Rhett's hair had once been the same golden blond that made Brandon such a cute kid.

"You're supposed to wear boxing gloves," he said gruffly.

"Oh." She shook her hand out again. "But you're not wearing them."

Brandon merely shrugged, then dashed his forearm against his temple in a vain attempt to wipe the sweat away.

"Let me guess. Dear old dad?" She gestured toward the bag. "I can find a black marker, if you'd like to draw a face on it."

She frowned and stroked her chin, pretending to seriously give it some thought, and was rewarded with Brandon's light chuckle.

"If, however, this bag is supposed to represent that sweet, friendly police officer who drove you home from the station the other night, I definitely don't want to know about it."

She paused and winked at the youth. "And no Magic Marker faces. I don't look good in black."

That earned her a full-blown laugh, but it didn't last long. Brandon's brows soon went back to their original position, creased low over his forehead.

She felt awkward, and was certain she looked

that way, as well. She leaned against a gymnast's horse and tried to act casual. But how, exactly, did one look casual with a teenage boy? "Want to talk about it?"

He licked his lips in preparation to speak, and Callie could tell by the expression on his face he was going to refuse to give more than a cursory answer.

"No pressure, kid," she said hastily, charging in before he could come up with a way out. "I just figured I already kind of know what's going on, so you wouldn't have to bring anyone else into this—" she paused and ran her fingers through the hair at the base of her neck "—*delicate* situation. I've been told I'm a wonderful listener. And since I'm definitely not going to jabber to your friends, I think I'm a pretty safe bet, confession-wise."

"Or talk to my dad?" he asked sharply.

She zipped her thumb and forefinger across her mouth. "My lips are sealed."

He blew out a frustrated breath. "Dad won't let me go out for the football team this year."

He punctuated his sentence with a quick *one-two* of his fists against the rough vinyl covering the bag. "Just because I stole one stupid shirt, he's going to ruin my whole life."

Callie knew his bruised knuckles must be really bleeding by now, and she inwardly cringed in sympathy, simultaneously amused by the teenager's overexaggeration of his dilemma. Then again...

"He's still pretty mad about the other night, huh?" She couldn't blame Rhett for being angry, but no one knew better than she that there were two sides to this story.

Brandon nodded.

Every sensitive nerve within her mind demanded she ask him why he pulled such a stupid stunt in the first place, but she was certain Rhett had already asked those very questions, possibly a number of times.

She doubted if he'd received a plain answer back. If his own father couldn't get anywhere with Brandon, why should she expect to? Rhett was a psychologist, for pity's sake.

Not only that, but she suspected the memory of those questions, and the disagreement that followed, were all a part of Brandon's frustration now.

She decided the best way to help everyone concerned was to keep listening, if Brandon wanted to keep talking.

It didn't take long to realize he needed, if not wanted, a listening ear.

"Dad said if I—" *punch three-four* "—don't get my act together—" *left hook to the middle* "—he's going to send me away—" *two swift right jabs* "—to a military boarding school."

Callie's stomach dropped into her toes.

Military school.

Was this some kind of horrendous nightmare, or was history repeating itself right before her eyes? She wanted to pinch herself and pray she woke up.

Her head spun, and she squeezed her eyes shut, trying to steady herself through the red rage pulsing through her.

"You okay?" For a kid, he sounded pretty mature. And pretty concerned. "You don't look so good."

If she looked as pale as she felt, there was no doubt in her mind she didn't look so good. Her mind urged her to run, but her body wouldn't cooperate, no matter how her insides screamed in panic.

"There you are," came a familiar, honey-rich voice from the hallway. "Church started a half hour ago, young man. Why aren't you—?"

Rhett cut his sentence short when he noticed

the tall, shapely blonde by his son's side, meticulously and attractively dressed in a straight black skirt and an oversize snow-white sweater.

Officer Brockman.

As feminine as she'd looked in the polyester police uniform, that wasn't half what her Sunday outfit did for her, accentuating her tiny waist and long legs.

Rhett's breath caught in his chest and stuck there, unmoving. Callie Brockman was absolutely, stunningly beautiful.

He was pleased to find her at church. Naturally, it would be nice to be working side by side with another Christian when it came to the juveniles under parole. Shared faith, common goals and beliefs, would make many parts of the job easier for both of them.

It was a moment more before he noticed Callie's eyes were closed, and her face was an odd, blanched color.

"Are you okay?" he asked, quickly moving to her side to take her arm. He gave his son a sharp I'll-deal-with-you-later warning glare. A father's look.

"Could you...I...could use a glass of water, please," she croaked.

"I'll get it." Brandon was off like a shot.

Officer Brockman's eyelids flickered open and she met his gaze briefly. Then, with a groan, she squeezed her eyes tightly shut again.

However brief the action, it was enough for Rhett to notice her pupils were wide and her eyes glassy, as if she were on the verge of fainting. He didn't know much about fainting females, and he wasn't real keen on learning about them now.

Had Brandon said or done something to make her so upset?

It had to be Brandon. Why else would his son be in such a rush to leave the scene? And if it was...

"Look, I'm sorry if Brandon did or said something to offend you," he said softly and firmly, deciding a frank apology was the best course of action.

He was preparing to dive into the side of his speech that he'd rehearsed long before he'd found Callie in the gym—the part where he apologized for his behavior the previous Friday night, and for rushing her out of his house and slamming the door on her without cause.

But she cut him short before he could get his thoughts together, her eyelids opening wide, and her silver-blue eyes glimmering in the reflection of the fluorescent lighting which filled the gym.

"If *Brandon* said something to offend me?" Her voice was unnaturally shrill, and sparks lit her eyes. "*Brandon* was a perfect gentleman, thank you very much."

Color had returned to her face, staining her cheeks a pretty pink.

"Which is more than I can say for you," she added, in what Rhett could only assume was for good measure.

"Look, I'm sorry," he began. "I don't—"

"Don't threaten your son with things you don't mean," she said, her voice softer now, though it hadn't lost its sharp edge. "You'll be so sorry if you send him away." Her eyes filled with tears.

Rhett was flabbergasted.

Send Brandon away? What was the crazy woman talking about?

Before he could say so much as another word, even to ask her what she meant by her unusual and unwarranted accusation, she wrenched out of his grasp, and dashed haphazardly, heels and all, out the side door of the gymnasium that led to the far parking lot.

Stunned into inertia, he stood agog and watched her leave, feeling as if he should do something, but not having the slightest notion what that something might be.

"Where's Officer Brockman?" Brandon had returned with a glass of water and looked every bit as surprised as Rhett felt.

"She left," Rhett answered, still feeling bemused.

Brandon's eyebrows shot up in surprise. "Why?"

Rhett bit out an astounded chuckle. "Your guess is as good as mine."

He watched the empty doorway for a moment more, then patted Brandon on the shoulder, noticing only now that his son was drenched with sweat, and was gripping the water glass he'd brought for Officer Brockman with hands that had bruised and bleeding knuckles.

As they were standing next to the still-swaying punching bag, Rhett inwardly grimaced. It didn't take a rocket scientist to figure out what Brandon was doing here.

And why.

His only question was how Callie had joined him, and for what purpose.

The insatiable guilt of fatherhood stabbed through him once again, and he prayed for wisdom and guidance.

"C'mon, son," he said gently, putting his arm around the boy's shoulders. "Let's clean up those hands, and then we can go worship God. In the smaller chapel. Alone." He paused, heaving a world-weary sigh. "I think we could both use a little prayer right now."

Chapter Five

A few days later, Callie was sifting through the mounds of paperwork left to her by the last juvenile parole officer. It was a lot to do, but her mind wasn't really on her work.

Rhett Wheeler was never far from her mind. Even if she'd wanted to, she couldn't avoid him forever. If she could, she'd bury her head in the sand ostrich-style, except that she'd be as equally obvious as the silly bird to the curious onlooker, never mind anyone involved.

She'd gone *way* beyond *open mouth, insert foot*. More like a song from her childhood that chimed through her mind, haunting her.

I'm being swallowed by a boa constrictor...
And I don't like it very much.

Oh, gee, he's up to my knee.
Oh, fiddle, he's up to my middle…
Oh, dread, he's up to my…

Yes, well, she got the picture. Loud and clear. In over her head, in every sense of the word.

For some unknown reason, Rhett Wheeler had brought out the worst in her—not that the *best* was anything to rave about, but her behavior with Rhett definitely went beyond the norm, even for her.

It was bad enough that she was as klutzy as a clown and twice as eye-catching. But despite everything, even the glaring warning sirens in her head that suggested any dealing with Rhett wasn't going to be in her best emotional interest, why did she find her heart stirring with attraction every time he was around?

Every time she saw him arrive at the station, she made a beeline for the ladies' room. *Chicken.*

When, oh *when* would she learn to mind her own business and leave the rest of the world alone?

"Phone for you, Callie," Bobby announced from the switchboard, stifling a yawn with the back of his hand. "Line five."

Callie sighed and scooped up the receiver,

punching line five more forcefully than she needed. "Officer Brockman."

"Callie, it's Rhett."

Her heart beat such a wild tattoo she wondered if it might give her away. She schooled her features, though she knew Rhett couldn't see her through the phone line. But she didn't want *anyone* to suspect what the mere honey-richness of Rhett's voice did to her insides.

"Rhett. What can I do for you?"

"We need to talk."

"Look, about the other day at church. What I said about Brandon—"

"No."

That one single, solid word from Rhett slammed her words to a halt in her throat.

"What I meant is that we need to meet and talk about my *caseload.* I'd prefer *not* to talk about my son." She heard him pause and inhale audibly. "Ever."

Any hope that Rhett had forgiven her big mouth and wanted to start over with a clean slate went skittering away like a family of mice after hearing the snap of a mousetrap. And right along with her disappearing hopes went her confidence that she could handle this situation without making another lethal blow to her ego.

She steadied her quivering hands on the edge of the desk. "Of course."

"Can you meet me at my office in an hour? It's inside the old field house at Fifth and Main."

"Sure. Okay."

"Good." He sounded gruff, and she wondered if his bad mood was her fault.

Maybe. But it *wasn't* her fault he was stubborn, she thought defensively. Or that he was, however unintentionally, driving his sixteen-year-old son down the path of no return.

She uttered a stiff goodbye and clamped the receiver down on its cradle.

"Now I remember why I'm still single," she muttered under her breath. "Men!"

Her mind brushed through to her other meetings with Rhett—and Brandon—untangling the snarls as best she could. Remembering the details about Brandon's situation was enough to strengthen her resolve against Rhett.

She wouldn't back down on her position where Brandon was concerned, for she well knew the inevitable conclusion of such a path, even if Rhett refused to see it. Brandon was too good a kid to lose to a stubborn man, even his father.

She would fight tooth and nail if it meant keeping father and son together. Single parenting was tough enough without creating extra issues, and that's exactly what Rhett was doing, whether he realized it or not.

There were differences between his situation and Colin's, to be sure. There was no doubt in Callie's mind that Rhett loved his son, or that he wanted the best for the boy. That in itself made what happened between Colin and her father as far different as east and west.

But Callie knew all too well what happened when a father alienated his son, even unintentionally.

She bit back her frustration, along with other emotions she refused to name or acknowledge, at not being able to change anything despite her best effort.

Rhett was right in one thing—it was none of her business. She shuffled the pile of papers nearest her, then sighed aloud and pushed them aside. She wasn't getting anything accomplished sitting here staring absently at her piles of paperwork, her mind a million miles away.

She might as well go see the man and get it over with. She wondered if tarring and feathering was still legal in Oregon.

"Rough day?" Bobby asked with a friendly smile.

She glared at her desk full of papers as if they were Rhett himself. "I'll say," she groaned. "I think I'll get out of here and go visit Rhett. My head is pounding like a jackhammer."

It couldn't get much worse than this, she thought, gathering her papers together and slipping them in an attaché.

Or could it?

Rhett leaned back in his chair and jammed his fingers through his thick hair, wondering absently if he ought to go in for a haircut. It was only one of a thousand distracting thoughts he'd encountered this morning.

For some reason, he found himself unable to concentrate on the case file in front of him, or anything else for that matter. Hearing the silvery alto of Callie's voice over the telephone wire was enough to drive any man to distraction, even without the clash between them.

A conflict over his *son*, of all things.

Something had set her off about him, but though he'd gone over and over their meetings in his mind, he still couldn't find a common link.

Why did she care what happened to Brandon?

Certainly none of the parole officers he'd known in the past got personal with their cases, or expressed their personal opinions on what was best in any given situation.

What difference did it make to Callie what kind of father he was? Who had died and named her Royal Queen of the Universe?

He clamped his jaw until his teeth ached from being ground together. What happened between Brandon and him was all his, partly Brandon's and *no* one else's business.

Most especially not the attractive, annoying, *maddening* Officer Brockman.

As if his thoughts had caused her to appear, Callie stood leaning her back on the door frame, staring at him with a bevy of questions in her eyes, not to mention the sparkle of amusement.

He blinked and looked at his watch. "You're early."

She strode forward, carrying two steaming paper coffee cups from the espresso stand. "We didn't set an exact time," she reminded him. "I didn't know your preference, so you can take your pick. A double shot of espresso, or a rich chocolate latte."

A peace offering?

He met her gaze squarely, but all he could read

in the glimmering depths of her silver eyes was a tenaciousness that made his breath catch in his chest.

Obviously she hadn't blown out her candle of resentment toward him, and he didn't know how to feel about that. Inwardly, he shook his head in frustration, but outwardly he only smiled.

What would Jesus do in this situation?

Lord, help me be the one to let go and get past the brick wall between us, he prayed silently. *Help me reach her with Your love.*

He cleared his throat. "I'll take the espresso. I could use a double shot right about now."

A wave of compassion washed over him as he left his burden of frustration on God's shoulders. It was a sure sign he was on the right track. He strengthened his resolve not to react to her anger, but rather to pierce through the stone fortress of her heart with the love of God, to find and help the woman beneath the shield of her antagonism.

Perhaps the grudge she carried on her shoulders had very little to do with what had happened thus far with his relationship with Brandon. Maybe nothing at all.

Now that he thought about it, this line of reasoning made a great deal of sense. She'd certainly come out of nowhere blasting him with both barrels.

Before she'd really had the opportunity to size him up.

Before she had time to form a rational opinion.

The psychologist in him switched into gear with a vengeance. Who'd hurt her, and why? Why was she so angry with so little provocation?

He took a sip of his espresso and sized her up, allowing this new information—a hunch, really—to affect his view of her. His mouth twitched into the hint of a smile when she dropped her gaze against his scrutiny.

"I…" she began, then faltered to a stop.

Standing to her full height and wearing a deliberate expression, she tried again. "Was there a particular reason you wanted to see me right away?"

"I'll show you what I do here, and then we can discuss our current caseloads."

He patted a foot-high pile of file folders for emphasis, every one of which was overflowing with colorful, legal-size papers.

A good foot more of juvenile delinquent activity than he wanted to see in John Day. Or anywhere else, for that matter. Juvenile justice was an odd lot at its best, and ineffectual at its worst.

The court system believed in rehabilitation of its youngsters, where there was no such system in place for adult offenders. Yet in the same breath, they locked kids away in detention centers that were little more than overglorified prisons, where the rough learned from the rough how to major in a life of crime.

The only real hope was in community service, which was where he came in. But he was only one man, and he could only do so much in the limited hours of each day he spent with the youth here.

Maybe Callie Brockman could help.

He shook himself back to the present and gestured to the door. "If you'll follow me, I'll show you the field house."

Callie didn't miss the excitement in his voice as he mentioned his work, and she admitted curiosity as to what he actually did in this big, dusty field house. It wasn't like any juvenile justice building she'd ever seen.

At first she'd thought it might be a detention center, and grimaced at what must be unspeakable surroundings.

But there were no electric fences here, no kids in the yard. So she'd explored a little bit on her own.

Not that she'd gained much by her self-guided tour. She'd noticed a number of odd pieces of equipment that looked like it was in some semblance of order, though she couldn't figure out for what.

Some pieces looked like the fences jump horses used in competition, only they appeared too small for an equine. Large, curved tubes that looked like they belonged behind a dryer, boarded A-frame ramps and thin bridges completed the course, along with a succession of plastic poles placed about twelve inches apart in a straight row.

Definitely not anything that looked like a human could use, even if he was putting the kids through their paces, she thought, amused.

Quite frankly, she couldn't make heads or tails of it, and she waited, intrigued, for his explanation.

She followed him through the odd assortment of apparatus to the far door, which she'd missed earlier; not that it would have mattered, as the door was locked.

Rhett rustled the keys at his waist until he found the one he wanted, then led her into a noisy kennel full of barking, whining, yapping dogs.

Dogs, she discovered as she looked from kennel to kennel, that came in every breed, size, color and shape, from the sleek-looking greyhound to a box-headed bull terrier.

Her first instinct was to balk and run, and for the first time, it wasn't Rhett making her want to flee. The muscles in her neck and shoulders hardened into stone as she worked through it mentally.

"Are you okay?" Rhett stepped forward. One gentle hand went to her elbow, and the other arm slipped around her waist, supporting her as if she were about to faint.

Despite the cold sweat breaking out on her forehead, she knew she wouldn't faint. Not Callie Brockman. A memory surfaced, and she fought to press it back.

"I'm fine." She stepped out of his grasp and crouched before the first kennel, where a lanky black Labrador retriever puppy circled in excitement.

"Hello, puppy," she crooned. She set down her latte and reached a tentative finger through the fencing, conquering her innate fear of dogs by the sheer force of her will.

Hearing her voice, the pup stopped chasing his tail and licked Callie's fingers where they curled through the chain-link fence.

She chuckled. "Don't tell me this little fellow is a juvenile delinquent!"

Rhett laughed and shook his head. It was the first time he'd cracked a genuine smile in her presence, and Callie's heart did a somersault.

He went from being handsome to knock-down-drag-out gorgeous with a single upward twist of his lips. Not only that, but he looked a good deal younger when he smiled, and his grin accentuated the attractive fan of laugh lines around his sparkling green eyes that Callie only now noticed. Her mind gratefully shifted gears, away from the dogs' din.

Maybe Rhett wasn't the ogre she'd made him out to be in her mind. Maybe she'd overreacted. Maybe Brandon had made up that nonsense about military school. Or maybe Rhett was just blowing off steam, and hadn't been seriously considering sending his son away.

Had she mistaken Rhett's intentions toward Brandon all along? With Rhett smiling down on her, it suddenly appeared a very real possibility.

For the first time all day, she relaxed, allowing the tension in her shoulders to unknot, and the coils in her stomach to unwind.

Rhett took another sip of his espresso and gestured to the Lab puppy. "Would you like me to take him out for you? His name is Merlin."

She nodded, trying to mirror Rhett's enthusiasm for his dogs. She hadn't much experience with puppies, but Merlin looked adorable. And safe. "How old is he?"

"Four months." Rhett lifted the catch to the kennel and allowed the puppy to wiggle past him.

"So he is a juvenile, after all. And so cute!" Merlin rubbed his head under her fingers, and she scratched obligingly.

"Do you show these guys?" She hadn't walked the whole length of the area, but she guessed he had a number of dogs by the noise being made by the dogs' barking. Probably begging for attention. The ruckus increased exponentially when they heard the golden tenor of Rhett's voice, coaxing Merlin to sit and stay.

She turned her attention back to the puppy, who was obeying Rhett's series of commands surprisingly well for such a youngster.

"I can't show them," he said, crouching beside her and play-wrestling with the puppy after he'd put the dog at ease. "Not a one of them is purebred."

Merlin had abandoned Callie in favor of Rhett, who was growling out of the back of his throat and teasing the pup incessantly. He spoke to the dog with the endearing, high-pitched voice men used with pets and babies, and Callie felt her throat catch in response.

"Well, I see you have one fan, anyway," she commented, punctuating her statement with another laugh.

Rhett nodded. "He knows where his next meal comes from."

He stood suddenly and touched Callie's elbow in order to help her rise to her feet. The contact was gentle and light, but it felt to Callie as if an electric current had passed between them.

She tried to swallow, then wet her dry lips with the tip of her tongue. Her heart stopped and started like an automobile with engine trouble.

He released his hold as soon as she was on her feet, but the imprint of his fingers on her bare arm remained, warm and soft.

Just like Callie's heart.

Chapter Six

Even after playing with Merlin, Rhett thought Callie looked distinctly uncomfortable within the kennel walls, and he was eager to learn why. His dogs were his world, and though Callie was polite, it was clear she was nervous. He wondered if she sensed the way the dogs picked up on her unspoken fear, making them louder and more boisterous than usual.

"You look a little nervous," he said, tentatively poking into her thoughts.

Callie grimaced and leaned against a steel post. "I am." Her gaze blanked as she became distant, then brightened when, he supposed, her thoughts regained the present.

She cleared her throat. "When Colin and I were eight—"

Her sentence dropped abruptly as the Doberman pinscher behind her lunged into the gate, teeth bared and growling ferociously.

Without thinking, Rhett bolted into action. "Baron, *platz*." The dog immediately dropped into a down position.

Baron was the one dog in his kennel he wouldn't introduce to someone afraid of dogs, at least not without warning. He hadn't realized it was Baron's kennel Callie had been leaning against, caught up as he was in the silver-blue of her gaze. "He doesn't usually—" he began, turning to Callie with an apologetic shrug.

His words froze on his tongue as he realized he was alone in the kennel area. Callie was gone.

Abandoning all thoughts of working through Baron's outburst, he took off in the direction he guessed she'd gone. Outside, into the fresh air.

Anywhere away from Baron. He should have guessed, should have known. He'd seen the little hints she'd been giving him—the startled looks, her beautiful eyes just a bit wider than usual. Her breath increasing as she entered the kennel area.

"Callie?" he called as he exited the building,

silently chastising himself as every kind of fool. "Callie? Are you okay?"

"Mmm."

He whirled around to where the sound came from, and found Callie leaning her shoulders securely against the dull, dented aluminum of the warehouse siding. Her arms were wrapped tightly around herself, and her eyes were wide with panic.

"You look like you've seen a ghost," he commented softly, moving forward until he could smell the sweet, musky scent of her hair. Wanting to comfort, he tentatively reached for her, caressing her bare arms with his palms. She shivered, though the fall afternoon was unseasonably warm.

Rhett's breath caught in his throat. He wanted to say something—anything—to reach her, to comfort her, but his mind drew a blank.

After an extended moment of silence, Callie shrugged away from his grasp. "I did see a ghost, in a way."

"How's that?" His voice sounded gravely even to his own ears, though for a completely different reason. His heart matched the beat of her pulse marking time on the tender skin at the base of her throat.

She was so beautiful. And so fragile. If his

chest grew any tighter, he thought it might burst, so completely were the deluge of bewildering emotions consuming him.

"Your...dog."

"Baron?"

"The Doberman. I...he..."

She turned away from him, but he couldn't let her move away. He stepped forward and wrapped his arms around her waist, firmly but gently leading her back into his embrace. He half expected her to reject his hug once again, but though she froze in place, she didn't break his embrace.

"My twin, Colin, and I were playing out on the front lawn. You wouldn't expect for a little boy to..."

"Colin?" he queried gently, assuming her thoughts had drawn back to what she'd attempted to explain earlier.

Heart in his throat, he pictured an eight-year-old Callie playing with her twin. "Go on."

"Colin had the football, and was running across the yard. I think I'd skinned my knee or something, because I was sitting on the porch instead of chasing him.

"All of a sudden, out of nowhere, this Doberman was running down the street. Running straight toward Colin."

She swirled around and buried her head in his chest, shivering from the memory. Rhett tightened his grasp and brushed her hair away from her face with the backs of his fingers.

"I yelled, but it was too late. The dog tackled Colin. By the time my dad came and chased him off, Colin had been bitten numerous times."

She pulled in a deep, unsteady breath. "He was in the emergency room for hours while they stitched him up. He still has a scar on his chin."

"Why didn't you tell me this before?" he murmured softly. Stroking her hair with decisively slow, even caresses, he silently encouraged her to slow her breathing.

Callie responded to his touch, much more than she cared to admit. It had been a long time since she'd been so close to a man, and Rhett wasn't just any man.

He was a man who could coax a story of her past from her, when all she wanted to do was forget. A man who was, in his own quiet, gentle way, helping her face an incident she'd thought she'd forgotten and moved beyond.

All this added up to the making of an outstanding psychologist, but Callie didn't want to think about that now, nor why he'd provoked such a response from her. She'd never been one to talk about herself, to reveal any more than absolutely necessary to get by.

For some reason, she could talk to Rhett. She looked up into his face, wanting to voice what their budding friendship meant to her, but every thought flew out of her mind when her gaze met and locked with Rhett's.

Her gaze dropped to his lips, then moved back up to his eyes, where she read the same conflict of emotions she felt in her heart. It was a thought, and it wasn't; a feeling, and more. Rhett's hint of a smile confirmed it a moment before he bent to capture her lips with his in the sweetest, warmest kiss she'd ever experienced.

His lips barely covered hers, yet they caressed her soul, reaching into her and coaxing a response. Conceding to his touch was the easiest, and paradoxically the most difficult move she'd ever made, she thought as she slipped her arms around his neck and pulled him closer.

His kiss became hers. No vicious Doberman, no memories of Colin, no fear of what was, or what might be. For the first time in years, Callie Brockman experienced a moment of true peace in Rhett's arms.

The threadbare executive office chair creaked as Rhett leaned backward, lacing his fingers behind his head and groaning aloud as he worked the kinks out of his neck and back.

He really wasn't the office type, but he compromised by promising himself a good workout after he was finished shuffling the monumental pile of paperwork that went along with his job.

With a grunt, he righted himself in the chair, the flats of his palms flush with the glass-covered desk.

It was bad enough that he was a half a month behind on paperwork, without being sidetracked by thoughts of a certain police officer who gave the words *true blue* an entirely new meaning.

Being a community service agent to John Day's delinquent youth was his penance—the way to dig his way out of the hole he'd fallen into and reclaim his life.

Callie wasn't a part of that, yet she'd changed his world in a single afternoon. And though Rhett hadn't seen or spoken with her for days, her presence was as strong here at the field house as if she'd just walked out the door.

He didn't expect her to visit the field house any time soon, given their past history and her innate fear of dogs. He'd have to work on that—coaxing her to give him and his dogs a second chance. His dilemma with Callie never left his mind for long—not while he was sleeping, and definitely not when he was working.

Every time he'd get a good start on his paperwork, his mind would slip back to that explosive moment with Callie when his lips touched hers. How could one kiss change so much?

He was as brain-dead as a lovesick teenager, with about as much tact. He was afraid when he saw her again, he'd drop to one knee and propose. Thank goodness there were no diamond stores in John Day, or he might just end up doing something so insane he'd regret it for the rest of his life.

It wasn't the first time the notion of marrying again had crossed his mind, but it *was* the first time he'd put a face to that vague, ghostlike image of the woman who'd fit the mold he and Brandon had made for themselves.

Callie Brockman.

What was so crazy about his thoughts was that she wasn't the type of woman he'd considered *marriage material* at all—at least not what he'd thought he and Brandon needed.

Brandon needed a mother figure, something akin to Mary Poppins, only set to the tune of a teenage boy's requirements. And Rhett needed a feminine perspective to give him a heads-up on his son's needs whenever he was blind to them. Lately, that was more times than he dared count.

Callie *had* given her very dogmatic opinion on the subject of his son on numerous occasions, but that wasn't quite what Rhett had in mind.

Rhett had—sort of—planned to remarry someday. He'd tossed the idea around a few times, but that was before Brandon got into trouble with the law.

Now, facing the rebellion of his own son and nobody on either side to run interference, it appeared doubly essential to find *Ms. Right.*

He creased his eyebrows low over his eyes.

He didn't know exactly what it is he was looking for in a woman, but Callie wasn't—*couldn't be*—whatever that was, even if the role was yet to be defined.

He pictured a plump widow woman with a cheery disposition and a sweet smile. Someone who baked her own bread and made homemade sugar cookies. Someone who'd put frilly, handsewn curtains in her kitchen.

And flowers. Cheerful, colorful fresh flowers, carefully and artfully arranged in a vase on the kitchen table.

Callie was nothing less than a gun-toting spitfire who turned his insides to mush. No matter how hard he tried, he couldn't picture her worrying about frilly curtains, never mind sewing them, and he didn't know why it mattered, anyway.

He chuckled at the picture forming in his mind—Callie sitting at a sewing machine, humming a hymn while she sewed the ruffles on her new gingham curtains.

True, she had a heartstoppingly sweet smile. When she smiled, which wasn't very often.

Cheery disposition? She'd hardly qualify as Mary Poppins in that category, or any other. Yet she intrigued him as no other woman had—not even Kayla, God rest her soul.

"So, like, I'm here already," growled a young man from the doorway.

Rhett swung toward the door and received a well-practiced blank stare in response to his welcome.

Don't know, don't care. That was how kids acted these days. He shifted through his papers, looking for his schedule book, which was somewhere in this monstrous pile. And even when he found the book, it took him an excruciating moment to flip through it and look up the information he needed to proceed.

"Lance?"

"Yeah. Who wants to know?"

Rhett worked to keep the tone of his voice even, to keep his expression from betraying him. He was used to dealing with teenage attitude.

Teenagers. Guys who thought they owned the world and knew everything about everything. But being king of the mountain left them a long way to fall.

He inwardly grimaced. Must be rough. He wished *he* knew everything—like how to stop these kids from getting into trouble in the first place.

Or at least how to cushion them from another fall. His own son most of all.

Rhett forced a smile as he stood, towering over the skulking youth in a conscious, if subtle, intimidation tactic. The kid might as well figure out right now where his attitude was going to take him.

"C'mon, son," he said, placing a gentle hand on the boy's bony shoulder and turning him around toward the door.

Lance shrugged out of his grasp, but Rhett continued, pretending not to notice. "We've only got an hour today. And we've got a mountain of work to do."

Chapter Seven

Callie turned the key backward in the ignition and shut the motor off, but didn't immediately exit her SUV. She stared wanly at the large, ugly aluminum-paneled warehouse and sighed.

This wasn't going to work. She leaned back, tossing her keys from one palm to the other and back again. As hard as it was to admit, even to herself, she was terrified of animals, especially dogs. She'd never owned a pet of her own, which made Rhett's obvious passion for his job something completely beyond her scope of experience.

There were cat people, and there were dog people. And then there was Callie. As usual, she didn't fit into any category. A paradox. An enigma.

A complete and total mess. And thinking about Rhett—about the kiss they'd shared—only made things worse. None of her defenses worked against the kindest man she'd ever met.

Had he been other than what he was, she would assume he'd taken advantage of her during a weak moment. At least then she could be angry, an emotion as familiar and comfortable to her as her pair of old, broken-in running shoes.

But that wasn't what Rhett had done, and she didn't know how to feel. He'd offered a bit of himself to comfort her, and she'd welcomed it with open arms.

If there was a problem, it was most certainly hers. How she was going to work with him on a continual basis without wanting to kiss him again was beyond her.

But wanting and doing were two different things. Surely she could keep one from becoming the other, couldn't she?

She wasn't so sure anymore. Her record wasn't good when it came to thinking before she spoke. Or kissed, in Rhett's case.

Truth.

He was a threat in a sweat suit. Or with his broad shoulders exaggerated by the cut of a sport coat like the one he wore for church, she mentally amended. Or in slacks and an oxford shirt like he wore for work.

She was in big trouble here.

Truth.

At least she could be honest with herself.

The primary reason Rhett Wheeler presented a big threat was not that he mishandled his relationship with his son, nor that they'd gotten off on the wrong foot initially. All that was child's play next to the real problem.

Rhett Wheeler made her socks roll up and down, despite her best efforts to ignore the obvious, that she was wildly attracted to the man.

She always thought she'd go for the Superman type, not Clark Kent in the flesh.

Rhett had shown her a whole new side to *Mr. Nice Guy.* Who would have known?

A laugh tickled her throat, the sound echoing through the vehicle. "You've got to laugh, or you'll cry," she said aloud, then shrugged her shoulders in answer.

She'd make this work, this working relationship with Rhett Wheeler. No more barbs—no matter how he set her off, intentional or otherwise. And definitely no more kissing.

As much as possible, she'd just ignore the man

and do her job. Ignore him as much as a woman could do with a man like Rhett.

With a quick, deep breath of air for courage, she exited the vehicle and marched determinedly toward the front entrance to the field house, her good intentions fresh in her mind.

Her attraction to Rhett was no longer an issue.

She hoped.

Her reaction to the dogs she couldn't vouch for...but a woman could only concentrate on so many problems at once.

As she approached, she heard the muffled sounds of male voices and decided to let herself in without knocking. It was a bit unconventional, especially for the small-town western mentality of each man to his own.

Privately, she hoped she'd have the opportunity to see Rhett in action, see the fruition of the community service methods he was so excited about, not having forgotten for one moment her last time visiting here with Rhett and his kennel.

As she let herself in, she spotted Rhett walking between the dog kennels, talking to each pup in turn. A young man with long, stringy hair of an indeterminate color followed at a distance, his hands crammed into the pockets of oversize, droopy jeans, a style currently the favorite among teenage boys in the area.

Rhett called to the boy, but he continued to hang back.

"Not afraid of dogs, are you, Lance?"

The boy squared his shoulders and took an aggressive stance, though Callie noticed he still stayed a good way from the dog kennels. "No way."

She could relate. It would take a minor miracle to get her near those kennels now.

Rhett merely smiled. Callie wondered if perhaps he enjoyed ruffling a few teenage tail feathers. Or did he not realize a flat-out lie when he saw one?

"Good thing for you," he said to the boy, his sparkling green eyes squinting into laugh lines. He gestured to the largest, slobberiest dog Callie had ever seen. "Because this fellow here is your new partner."

Any doubt Callie might have had that the boy might be hanging back because he was intentionally trying to be churlish or uncooperative, however much he might have been both, flew out the window on a breeze.

That kid was scared stiff.

Rhett flipped the gate open and called the dog

to him, acting and looking as if there were nothing out of the ordinary in this situation. Did he really not see?

In the same instant, the boy plastered himself against the opposite kennel, only to lunge back wildly when the dog in the kennel behind him jumped up on the fencing and barked in excitement.

Callie shivered, only marginally tempering her own fear of animals. Fear for herself as much as for the boy. Memories of Colin surfaced, along with the guilt she'd never been able to quench. She gripped her attaché case with two fists.

Rhett restrained the large dog by the collar. Callie's eyes widened as she got a good look at the monstrous, slobbery dog, if a dog was, in fact, how that animal could be classified.

It reminded Callie more of Bigfoot than a puppy, though that's what Rhett called it. At least as tall as Rhett's waist, it sported a muscular, fawn-colored body that was only superseded by his oversize head and colossal jaws.

The dog's head reminded Callie of a game she'd played as a child, where she assembled various multicolored plastic animal bodies with an equally assorted number of animal heads.

She'd spent many happy hours making Eleraphs and Rhinoroosters.

This dog was such a creature—definitely one of the most unusual of God's creations she'd ever laid eyes on. And the young man appeared to agree with her assessment.

The dog was large, slobbery and nasty. She could see the whites of his eyes even from where she was standing, and the boy was a good deal closer. No wonder the kid was still struggling to regain his composure.

What was Rhett thinking? He appeared immensely insensitive, which went against everything she knew about him. Confusion washed over her.

This massive brute was a far cry from the Labrador retriever puppy he'd introduced her to the other day. Giving the kid a taste of his own medicine, maybe?

She restrained herself once again, this time from darting forward to lend the boy a hand. This was Rhett's territory, and though it went against the grain, Callie trusted him enough to keep watching without interfering.

Whatever Rhett's strategy, it appeared to be working. In fact, it would be almost laughable, if the poor kid didn't look so terrified, *and* if she was absolutely certain Rhett meant it as a joke.

But she wasn't certain of anything at the moment. Rhett certainly *looked* serious. Determined. And calm.

"I'm not touching no dog," the youth spouted, flipping his hair out of his eyes with a jerk of his chin.

Rhett merely shrugged. "Up to you, son. You can pick up trash along the highway if you want."

The youth scowled.

Rhett met him stare for stare, then flicked his glance in her direction. Their gazes met for only a moment, but that was all she needed to see into the soul of the man, and what she saw made her world spin.

She read a myriad of emotions in his gaze. She half expected the hard edge, disillusionment or polite unconcern she'd so often seen in the social workers in Portland, but she found only gentleness. Strength tempered by compassion.

A man of steel masquerading as mild-mannered. Or maybe the best combination of what both Superman and Clark Kent had to offer.

"Lance, I'd like to introduce you to Bear, our resident mastiff." Rhett's mild tenor was as warm as honey, and Callie swallowed with difficulty.

Apparently, though, Rhett's voice wasn't quite as effective on the boy as it had been on her. Lance merely shrugged, his eyebrows a thick, dark line dashed over his eyes.

He wasn't giving an inch, whether from anger or fear. Callie suspected it was a little of both. And Rhett knew exactly what he was doing.

"So?" Lance blurted, as belligerent as ever.

To Callie's amazement, Rhett didn't bat an eye, even when she herself had, for a moment, forgotten her fear of dogs in response to the boy's antagonism.

She'd only been watching for a few minutes, and she was frustrated beyond belief. How did Rhett stay so composed? How'd Rhett know to make the right match, of dog to kid and kid to dog? There was a lot more to this therapy dog business than she'd first believed.

And with what she'd seen so far, she was admittedly impressed. Lance wasn't making Rhett's job easy on any count, but Rhett took it in stride, never missing a beat as he spoke to the boy.

Then again, the mastiff was on Rhett's side. All things being equal, she'd vote for the dog.

"Bear wants to shake your hand."

The youth's eyebrows popped up so high they

were lost under the stubborn lock of hair that fell down over his eyes. "No way."

Again, Rhett merely shrugged. "Your call. If you don't like Bear, I can always..."

He left the sentence dangling, and Callie smiled. Rhett knew *exactly* what he was doing.

"No," Lance said after an electrical silence. "I'll take the stupid dog."

Rhett didn't quite smile, but the laugh lines reappeared around his eyes, which were glimmering with amusement. "I think you'll find Bear to be smart enough for you."

He ruffled the dog's floppy ears. "Lance, meet Bear. Bear...Lance."

The boy tentatively held out his hand, and was rewarded when the big dog lifted his paw for a shake.

Lance chuckled, a foreign and unexpected sound to Callie's ears.

"Well, whadda ya know?" Lance murmured, cocking his head and visually relaxing.

"You don't have a dog?" Rhett queried gently, though the answer was obvious enough.

"No," said the boy, scratching Bear under the chin, and laughing when the dog flopped over onto his back so Lance could scratch his belly.

"My mom never—" He cut himself short with a scowl, though he didn't stop scratching the dog.

Rhett nodded in encouragement, as though he'd been witness to a giant breakthrough with Lance, rather than producing a single statement that told Callie, and no doubt Rhett, much more than if the boy had completed his awkward sentence.

"Bear likes to chase sticks," Rhett said, slipping a lead on the dog's collar. "Think you can handle that?"

The boy shrugged a shoulder as if he didn't care either way, but his eyes were shining with excitement.

With a nostalgic smile, Callie wondered how long it had been since Lance had anything to be excited about. What Rhett was doing here was nothing short of a miracle.

"Out back, then," Rhett instructed gruffly. "Keep Bear inside the fence, please."

Callie's heart leapt into her throat and froze there. Was it really safe to allow the young man and the dog to be alone together? Rhett didn't appear concerned, so she allowed the thought to pass untested, though not without some effort.

"Callie," he said, waving her over as he began adjusting the chain on one of the kennel gates. "Glad you could make it today."

She smiled, her breath catching in her throat as a fluttery feeling washed over her. She supposed it had something to do with seeing another side to Rhett, a mysterious combination of strength and gentleness that was uniquely masculine.

She shifted mental gears as quickly as possible, the clutch grinding. "I have to say that was an astonishing display."

Rhett cocked his head and stopped wrapping the chain around the kennel. "How's that?"

"The boy and that...*dog.*"

He crooked a grin. "Bear will be good for Lance."

"If you say so." Callie shook her head. "Though I don't understand why you'd pair a kid who is so obviously afraid of dogs with *Bear.*"

She shivered despite her best efforts. Rhett's glance was full of compassion, and heat rushed to Callie's cheeks. Would she ever be free of her fear?

If only...

Chapter Eight

Rhett gestured toward his office. He felt oddly pleased by Callie's interest in the dogs, especially considering how frightened she was of them. "I'd be happy to explain the rationale behind my choice, but I'm sure we'd both be more comfortable in my office."

Callie nodded, looking distinctly relieved by his suggestion. He held the door and allowed her to precede him. As she passed, her gaze rose to his, a question in her eyes. He didn't know the answer. He couldn't think straight with her soft, musky scent tantalizing his senses.

"Please sit down," Rhett offered, covering his discomfiture with a gesture of courtesy. "Have you eaten? I've got some doughnuts. And there's soda in the fridge.''

''Anything chocolate works for me.''

''Soda?''

''Water, if it's bottled and cold.''

Rhett reached into the small fridge for a bottle of water for Callie and an orange juice for himself, then flipped open the box of doughnuts on the shelf, selecting a maple bar and a chocolate éclair.

He set the éclair before her and took a bite of the maple bar, settling himself on the corner of the desk with his weight on one hip.

''I have to know why you gave that kid such a big dog,'' she said, gesturing back to where the teen had been, picking up the conversation where they'd left off. ''I mean, it was perfectly obvious even to me that the poor boy was scared to death.''

Rhett grinned, feeling like a schoolboy whose girlfriend had seen him make the winning touchdown at a football game. ''I thought I'd give the kid someone his own size to pick on.''

Callie laughed in delight. ''You know, I was thinking that very same thing when I was watching you.''

"Were you, now?" he asked, feeling oddly pleased by the notion.

Their gazes met and locked for a moment that was both a second and an eternity. He thought his heart stopped dead in his chest. At any rate, his lungs were burning from sudden lack of use.

Callie broke eye contact first, turning aside and taking a bite of éclair. He didn't know whether to feel offended or relieved. That was the problem. He didn't know *how* to feel.

He cleared his throat and took a sip of his juice, trying with debatable success to regain his equilibrium.

After a long pause, he attempted to regain the easy camaraderie they'd had minutes earlier by returning to the subject of Lance and Bear. "Bear is the least aggressive dog in the kennel."

Understandably, she looked unconvinced.

"Really," he insisted. "Mastiffs are big and rough-looking with teddy-bear hearts."

Callie gave him an odd look, a mixture of surprise and something he couldn't put his finger on. "As opposed to Dobermans?"

Rhett pursed his lips in thought. Instinctively, he knew his next words were do or die, and he wanted to say the right thing. "Callie, there aren't bad dogs. Only bad people. The Dobie who attacked your brother was probably taught that aggressiveness by his owner.''

"Do you think?" Callie retorted.

Rhett chose to ignore her animosity. "I took Baron from the pound when no one else would take him.''

"Why am I not surprised?"

"I won't ever be able to use Baron in the therapy dog program, but hopefully he'll mellow out enough to find a new home through the Doberman rescue foundation. He needs a lot of love and work to get over his aggressive tendencies, but he'll get there.''

"You sound pretty confident.''

"You'd be amazed,'' he said through a tight throat, "at what love can do.''

Her jaw dropped in surprise, but she quickly closed it again. He plunged on while he still had the advantage. "Back to poor Bear—he was scheduled for doggie death row. Would have been a waste.''

He shook his head, remembering the many dogs—and kids—he couldn't help. That was a part of his burden as a social worker, and a therapy dog worker, that he could never quite unload.

But at least he could, and did, help Bear. Eventually, he'd help Baron, as well.

And, Lord willing, Lance.

Callie appeared to be following his train of thought. "And Lance?" She spoke softly, with a hint of a catch in her throat. He wondered if she were feeling the same effects he was whenever they were together.

Again, he plunged on. "Lance is just another kid looking for attention any way he can get it." The brick in his chest softened as he looked out the window, watching a smiling Lance toss a stick for the large, lumbering dog to retrieve. "It's only a matter of time until they turn to crime, when nothing else does the job."

He shook his head, wishing he didn't sound fatalistic. "I try to give kids like Lance positive experiences with people—and animals."

Callie nodded. "It's been my experience that those who mistreat animals often mistreat people, as well. Not that I've been around that many animals," she amended.

He narrowed his eyes on her as pain flitted across her face. Without making a conscious decision to do so, he reached out for her, brushing his knuckles against the sweet softness of her right cheek.

Meeting Callie had been the parallel of getting to know a tornado on a personal level—a hard-edged woman who swung defensively at every turn and wore her attitude like a turtle wore his shell.

But then, she'd probably learned from the school of hard knocks. It couldn't be easy to be a lady cop, not under the best of circumstances, and he suspected hers weren't.

Her delicate skin was like the brush of rose petals under his touch. What a shocking contrast. There was definitely more to this woman than met the eye. Not for the first time, he was interested— *very* interested—in getting to know the woman behind the emotional fortress she'd so securely erected around herself.

No time like the present.

"You sound as if you're speaking from experience," he queried gently, ready to drop the subject on the spot if she didn't feel inclined to talk about it.

For the slightest moment, she leaned into his caress, and he caught his breath at the sensation, like warm maple syrup drizzling over pancakes.

But the next moment, she turned away, standing so suddenly her chair spun on its coasters. "We weren't talking about me," she returned, her voice raw with emotion.

Apparently he'd hit a nerve.

"Right," he agreed immediately, dropping his hand to the corner of the desk.

"Lance," he murmured, more to remind himself of a safe topic than to remind her.

"Lance," she repeated, as if that lone word were a lighthouse in a storm.

"I'll train Lance with Bear for a few weeks, until he's comfortable with the dog, and vice versa. That's what all the equipment is for—dog training. And kid training."

He flashed her his most charming smile. "When I think they're both ready, I'll take him with me to a nursing home or a hospital. Dogs are a big hit in the pediatric ward."

Callie's silvery eyes widened noticeably. "They let you take *dogs* into hospitals?"

He nodded. "Sure. My dogs make the kids smile, and forget about being in the hospital for a while."

"But isn't that unsanitary? I'd think the nurses on duty would be pitching fits."

His grin widened. "Some of them do. But not those who've studied dog therapy, or seen it in action."

She nodded, her focus completely on his words.

"Of course we don't visit intensive care or those with infections, but there are whole wards full of cancer patients, especially in the kids' ward.''

"Children?"

He pinched his lips together and nodded.

It wasn't something he liked to think about, but it came along with the job. It was undeniably difficult to see those little ones suffering and dying from a terminal illness and know he could do nothing about it, except give them a moment of relief through a smile or a laugh.

He could definitely relate to the sheen of moisture in Callie's eyes, even if he kept his own feelings locked deep inside.

"I never get tired of seeing the way a surly kid destined for juvie hall can change once he's been given something meaningful to do with his time."

He hoped the sudden gear switch sounded natural, but he could tell from Callie's expression she suspected what he was doing—carrying the conversation so she could pull herself together.

In fact, Callie knew exactly what Rhett was doing, and appreciation for his thoughtfulness nearly overwhelmed her already overstimulated senses. Light and kindness blazed from his eyes, and she wondered at the source. She didn't know what to call it, but whatever it was, she liked it.

"I'd never heard of therapy dogs until I met

you—er, I mean, moved to John Day," she commented, sliding over her blunder.

He nodded enthusiastically. "The use of therapy dogs is a relatively new practice in the field. The great part about it is that it benefits everyone involved, from the elderly ladies and gentlemen in the nursing home to the delinquent youth on the other side of the leash."

Callie was genuinely interested, and was becoming more sold on the method with every word Rhett uttered.

"And the dogs love all that attention, of course. They're incredible to watch. They instinctively appear to know why they're there. It's a riot to watch them preen and primp at being the center of attention.

Callie laughed softly. "Somehow, I can't see Bear primping and preening."

"Showing off, then."

"I must admit, it sounds fascinating."

"It is." Passion lined his voice, and Callie recognized the rise of envy as what it was.

If only *she* had something to believe in so fervently. Even becoming a cop wasn't like that for her. She wasn't fulfilling the desire of her heart with her work. It was more the instinctual reaction of an animal backed into a corner with nowhere to go—fighting back because it was the only thing she could do to save herself.

"Callie?"

"Hmm?" she answered absently.

Rhett chuckled. "I asked you a question."

"Oh. I'm sorry." Her cheeks burned.

"Would you like to go out with me sometime?"

Callie drew in a quick, surprised breath.

"I mean, not *go out* go out, but come with me when I'm visiting the hospital or a nursing home with the therapy dogs."

Her heart, which had moments before been doing a victory dance in her throat, dive-bombed into her toes and sat there like cement.

She could feel the color in her face rising. Of course Rhett was talking about work. How could she possibly have interpreted it any differently?

And yet she had, for one brief, wonderful second.

She composed her features automatically. Her reply hovered on the edge of her tongue, but her voice deserted her when she needed it most.

After an awkward moment, her voice returned. "Yes, I'd be glad to go with you." Thankfully, her voice didn't squeak.

He smiled widely at her answer, looking as pleased as a boy with a frog in his pocket.

She laid a hand on his muscular forearm, enjoying his enthusiasm for his life and work, and, deep in her heart, hoping some of it might rub off on her. She couldn't remember the last time she'd felt so enthusiastic about something. Or some*one*.

"You know, Rhett, what you're doing here is incredible. It's like a miracle or something."

She felt like a cat choking on a fur ball, and the bitter laugh that suddenly burst from the doorway made her swallow it whole.

"Yeah, right," said Brandon as both Rhett and Callie whirled around toward the entrance.

Callie felt a pump of adrenaline, as if she'd been caught doing wrong, though of course that wasn't the case. Brandon's glare made her feel as if she had; and Rhett, too.

"That's my dad. *Incredible*."

Brandon was quivering with anger, his face a mottled red under his honey-gold hair and dark eyebrows. He looked as if he were ready to burst with rage.

And the next moment, he did, slamming his fist into the drywall and putting a hole clean through the wall next to the door.

Callie turned to Rhett, whose jaw was dropped,

either in astonishment or in prelude to speech, though no words came from his effort.

She struggled for words herself, wondering what she should say or do.

One moment later it was too late to do anything at all.

Brandon was gone.

Chapter Nine

Callie looked as if she'd suddenly become enamored of the condition of her fingernails.

Even so, he felt her subversive gaze, and knew she was watching him intently. He knew she felt, as he did, the thick, electrical tension in the air that rivaled that of a thunderstorm.

No doubt she was waiting to see if he'd fly off the handle, as he'd done in the past—at least when she was present. Funny, there was a time when he banked on his rock-solid self-control. Now he couldn't even trust himself.

But maybe that was the problem here. He wasn't in control, and it bothered him incessantly.

God was in control.

His mind acknowledged the fact, but the rest of him rebelled. Where was God in all this?

Rhett couldn't be a good father to Brandon unless the heavenly Father deemed to help him out. And right now it sure didn't feel like God was anywhere close by.

Not with him, and not with Brandon.

Rhett folded his arms, his palms flat against the reassuring solidness of his chest. His lips and brows were parallel lines on his face as he glared at the doorway through which his son had disappeared.

"I'm sorry you had to see that," he said softly, his voice raw.

Callie placed a hand on his shoulder and cleared her throat, but no words came. Her mind blanked as she fished for something encouraging to say.

Despite their bad beginning, she now considered him a friend, and she was glad to be here now to help, though she wasn't sure if her presence was welcome or not.

"I—I know you and Brandon aren't on the best of terms right now. But I wouldn't worry about it too much, if I were you. I'm guessing all parents of teenagers go through this awkward stage, in one form or another."

Rhett grunted his assent. "Do you think?"

She nodded and brushed the hair back from his temple with the tips of her fingers in a feminine gesture that was old as time itself.

"Not that I'm an expert, or anything," she added.

He slumped against the desk, palms down. "I don't know what to do with him anymore. We used to get along great, when he was a kid."

"He still is a kid," Callie reminded him gently. "Have you tried talking to him?"

He burst into a bitter laugh. "I've tried. It's like I'm not speaking English or something. And I sure don't know what language he's speaking. I just don't get it."

"Too bad colleges don't give a course in Teen-ageeze."

He straightened and turned to look at her, a half grin on his lips. "Maybe I ought to bottle it. I could make millions. If I could just figure it out myself, for one lousy moment."

Callie's chuckle caught in her throat. "Are you going to go after him?"

Rhett glanced at the doorway and then back at her. "Should I?"

She shrugged, feeling pinned to the spot. "I can't tell you what to do."

As soon as the words were out of her mouth, she wished them back. What had she been doing all along where Rhett and Brandon were concerned, if it wasn't telling him what *she* thought he should do?

But now she knew better. Much better.

With every passing day, she realized just how much she *didn't* know about the world, never mind about Rhett Wheeler's heartrending situation.

And Brandon—how had she ever thought she could help him? What little she knew about teenagers was from her own experience, and that of her twin brother.

She had no idea whatsoever if the male adolescent experience even remotely resembled what she'd been through, which quite frankly hadn't been that great.

Colin had been sent away before his hormones had kicked in full force. She'd felt helpless then, and she felt equally helpless now.

All she did remember from her teenage years were tears and pain. *The best years of my life? I don't* think *so.*

There was Colin, of course. But look how that turned out.

Rhett quirked one dark eyebrow, and she was

glad to see a sparkle of amusement back in his green eyes. "Not even some advice?"

She barked out a laugh. "I think I've given you enough of *that* to last a lifetime."

"Yeah, well, you were probably right." He frowned, his eyes turning brown with emotion. "On all counts."

"No," she denied with a vehement shake of her head. "I was sticking my nose where it didn't belong. And I'm officially unsticking it as of now."

"Should I go after him?"

She sighed. He wasn't making this turning-a-new-leaf stuff easy on her.

"If you were me, I mean. What would you do?" His expression continued to fluctuate between a scowl and a smile that slipped from time to time, reminding her how serious the situation truly was.

She ran a hand across her chin. "He's trying to make a point," she said, thinking aloud.

"Then I should go after him."

"But he's really upset, so he's not going to listen to you right now."

"Then I should give him his space until he comes to me."

"If he's really looking for attention, which I think he is—"

"Callie!" Rhett groaned. "You're not helping me out here."

She shrugged. "I think…"

"Okay, okay. I'm going after him."

She nodded in agreement. "If you give me your keys, I'll lock up for you, and drop the keys back at your place later today."

She looked around, then frowned. "You'd better put Bear away before you leave."

He grinned, his eyes sparkling with mischief. "Not afraid of a dog, are you?" he teased.

She nodded emphatically. "Absolutely. Without a doubt, terrified out of my wits."

"Funny," he answered, scrubbing a hand across his cheek. "I didn't think you were afraid of anything."

Brandon was right where Rhett thought he'd be, sulking in his room, stretched out across his water bed with his stereo blasting holes in the ceiling.

Rhett knocked twice, then entered on his own when Brandon didn't respond.

"We need to talk." He tried not to let his anxiety show, nor raise his voice, despite the noise of the stereo.

He had to keep the upper hand. He was Brandon's father. And he had to make things right.

Brandon rolled to his back and opened a magazine, holding it up like a shield.

"I know you can hear me, so you just listen, and I'll talk."

He took a deep breath. Brandon really knew how to push his buttons, and he was pounding on them at the moment. Once again, frustration was taking the upper hand.

"No more scenes like the one today, okay?"

"Yes, *sir*. Whatever you say, *sir*," snapped Brandon caustically.

"Knock it off, buster. I should be grounding you for this. Until you're thirty, if I had my way."

As soon as the words were out, Rhett clamped his jaw closed and mentally pounded himself in the head.

Once again, Brandon had provoked him to anger; and Rhett, in turn, had blown things completely out of proportion.

Lord, help me here! He prayed, feeling apprehensive and volatile. *I'm blowing it. Again. Make me a better father, You, who are the Father of the world. You must know what it's like to deal with children who won't listen to You.*

That thought sobered him.

"Talk to me." It was more of a request than a command, and he hoped his son took it that way.

Brandon didn't budge, and Rhett couldn't see his face from where he was standing, so he had no idea what his son was—or wasn't—thinking.

"Brandon, talk to me." He was nearly begging now, and it was making him angry. How was he supposed to help his kid if Brandon wouldn't even give him the time of day?

Taking another deep breath, he knelt by the edge of the bed. "Will you pray with me?"

That appeared to have caught his son off guard, because he put the magazine down in his lap. "You want to pray?"

"Sure."

"To confess my sins?" Brandon queried, the bitterness of his tone slicing into Rhett like a knife.

Rhett shook his head adamantly. "No, son. Not to confess *your* sins. To confess *mine*."

Chapter Ten

I didn't think you were afraid of anything.

Rhett's words echoed in her mind during the short drive from the field house back to her home. Taunted her, almost, though she knew he'd been joking.

All her life she'd kept herself aloof, except for Colin. And now Rhett. Under his inspection, her tough-cop facade was as flimsy as the thinnest veneer.

She didn't want him to discover the truth about her—that she was afraid of everything, and Rhett most of all. There were more sparks between the two of them than the skies of Oregon on the Fourth of July, and she was completely and utterly terrified of going up in flames.

As she pulled down her street, she was surprised to find a polished hunter-green, full-size sports utility vehicle parked in her driveway. She recognized the make and model of the vehicle, but not the license plates, which she thought might be out of state.

Maybe one of her neighbors was having company stay over, though why they'd park in *her* driveway was a mystery.

Curious, she pulled up next to the curb in front of her house and stepped out of her car.

"Callie."

Her world immediately tilted and began to spin.

She grappled for something solid, and clutched at the hood of her car for support.

The man's voice was a soft, lilting tenor as he said her name. A voice she'd heard before, knew every bit as well as her own.

Even if she hadn't heard him speak in years.

Even if the last time she'd seen him they were both sixteen.

"Colin."

A single word. And a lifetime of emotion.

She looked out over the hood of her car to the house across the way, unable to turn and face her long-lost brother, afraid he might fade into the mist if she turned around. The blood that was momentarily frozen in her veins was suddenly rushing to her face.

"How's it going, sis?" How well she remembered the constant tone of lightness and laughter in his voice. It was deeper than when he was sixteen, but it was definitely Colin.

"How's it going?" She was yelling, but she neither knew, nor cared. "You disappear off the face of the planet for ten years and then you waltz in here as casual as all get-out to ask me *how it's going?* What right do you have?"

"I officially waive all my rights." His voice was right behind her ear.

Startled, she whirled around, continuing to grip the hood of her SUV.

Colin embraced her, holding her tight while she pummeled his back with her fists. He didn't offer a word of explanation, and he didn't attempt to stop her outburst of emotion, or her abuse.

"You could have called, Colin, even if you didn't want to come home." That she was talking about a time eleven years in their past was irrelevant. Hot tears streamed down her face, but she ignored them.

Just as quickly as it had appeared, the fight abruptly shattered, leaving her drained and sobbing into her brother's shoulder. "You could have called."

"I know. I should have called. But I was so angry. I felt betrayed. And then it had been so long, I was afraid." He spoke softly, hesitantly. "After a while, it was easier not to call at all."

She stepped back, brushing the tears off her cheeks with her palms. The world was still spinning, but she was beginning to be able to link one coherent thought with another.

Maybe she'd eventually be able to think this through like a rational individual. Until then, she'd have to do the best she could.

Colin was here. He'd grown into a handsome heartbreaker of a man, with broad shoulders and his silver-blond hair cut in a military style that accented his dress-white uniform.

"Dad said you'd probably gone off and joined the Marines," she said, sniffling into the handkerchief he offered. "I guess he was right."

Colin smiled, but his blue eyes were sad. Unlike Callie's silver-blue, her twin's eyes were a wide, clear sky-blue. "Half right," he replied briskly, and Callie wondered whether that was from his experience in the military, or from the subject at hand. "I joined the navy."

"The *navy?*" The more Colin talked, the less

sense he made. "But I thought you hated military school!"

"Oh, I did," was his immediate reply. "More than you'll ever know."

His voice took on a hard edge, and Callie wished she hadn't been quite so forthright in quizzing him about his past.

"I may as well have been sent to a halfway house, Callie. In fact, in many ways, I would have preferred it. Being sent away from your family— from your twin sister..."

He didn't bother to finish his sentence, but forged on into new territory. "Dunworthy Academy was just as much of a prison as any jail cell could have been for me. Maybe worse, sometimes. A lot of times."

"Then why did you go and join the navy?" He wasn't making any sense, and she ached with every part of her being to understand.

It had been so long. Too long.

Colin looked away, off toward the sunset. "I wanted to disappear. The navy offered me an easy out."

She frowned, unable to keep her hurt feelings from showing. "You obviously liked it well enough to have made it a career."

He squared his shoulders and nodded, his

mouth quirking into a half smile. It was an achingly familiar gesture, and though she hadn't seen it in years, it worked on her as it had when she was a child, and she instantly forgave him, just as she had always done.

Stubborn, mule-headed Colin, running off to join the navy just to spite their father. She couldn't say that it came as a total surprise.

"You couldn't think of anything better to do?" The sentence was spoken as an accusation, and she gestured to his uniform.

His jaw tightened until she could see the pulse beating at the corner of his freshly shaven cheek. But amusement sparkled in his eyes, so she knew he wasn't *really* angry.

"I can understand your reasons behind joining the navy," she coaxed, not giving him a chance to answer between her comments.

"I'll even admit my part in it. I should have gone to your graduation, no matter what Dad said. Nevertheless—"

He opened his mouth to speak, but she held him off with a wave of her hand. "*Nevertheless*, I fail to understand why you made the military your career if you hated it so much, *or* why you suddenly decided to show up on my doorstep after all these years."

She leveled him with a glare. "Two simple questions. Why the navy? And why come home now? Did you develop a conscience on one of the ships of yours?"

That last was spontaneous, but she wasn't sorry she said it.

"The navy has been good to me, Callie," he explained patiently.

Callie balked at his tone, sensing condescension there. "Oh, yeah. Navy's family, right?"

A pained look crossed his face, and he sighed deeply. "I guess I had that coming."

"What did you expect, Colin?" The anger of many years of holding her emotions deep inside her overcame her good sense.

She began shaking uncontrollably both inside and out. It was as if something had snapped within her heart. "Hey, brother, welcome home! Been a while."

"No. Of course I didn't think... I hoped that we... Oh, I don't know."

"Well, I do." She straightened up and glared at her twin. "You can march your fancy, spit-shined shoes and fine military uniform elsewhere. I'm not interested in renewing old *acquaintances*."

Without another word, she lifted her chin and

walked past him toward the front door of her house with as much dignity as a woman who'd just had her world turned upside down could muster.

"Acquaintances? Callie, listen to me!"

She held one hand in the air, palm outward. "I don't want to hear anything you've got to say."

"Callie!"

"Save it for someone who cares, Colin." She wasn't angry so much any more as resigned to the inevitable.

"I don't believe you're turning me away like this," Colin protested. "I came all the way from Midway Island just to talk to you. Do you know how many hours of standby plane travel that is? Don't cut me off like this without letting me explain."

Despite her best intentions, she whirled on him, her veneer cracking. "Explain? I thought you were already finished *explaining*."

She turned her back on him again, though she didn't continue the path to her front door. In a softer voice, she continued. "I'm not the one who cut our ties, Colin. I didn't run off without a word."

"I can explain that."

"Maybe I don't want you to explain."

"Callie—" he began.

She cut him short. "Do you have any idea what I went through those first few months, trying desperately to find you? I didn't have the money to hire a private investigator as a poor kid working her way through college. But believe me when I say I tried every other option I could think of."

She blew her air out in a big huff. "I even got religious for a while. I prayed my heart out, asking God to bring you home to me. But He didn't answer, Colin. I don't even think He heard me."

"He heard you," Colin replied, his voice cracking with emotion. "God heard you." He stepped forward and took both her hands in his. "God is why I'm here."

"Oh, I see. Of course. Why didn't I realize that earlier? You've got God's stamp right on your forehead. Heaven's post office isn't very efficient, is it?"

She didn't care that she sounded cynical. She *was* cynical.

Colin wasn't charging back into her life because God was answering her prayers. She'd stopped praying a long time ago. "He must have gotten behind on His requests. Or maybe I'm just not real high on His list of priorities."

"Callie, don't."

"No, *you* don't. I don't want to hear any more."

He scrubbed his fingers across his scalp, ruffling the short tips of his hair and ruining his impeccable military image.

"Do you remember back when we were schoolkids, and we went to that vacation Bible school where everyone dressed up like Bible times?"

"Sure," she answered, wondering where he was going with the question. It seemed an odd thing to bring up at the moment, and she definitely wasn't in the mood for games.

"Do you remember anything...*special* that happened while we were there?"

She glared at her twin, letting him know she wasn't overjoyed by his line of questioning, but nonetheless, she found herself searching the recesses of her mind for something, anything, she might say in reply.

Colin grinned.

"What?" she asked, annoyed.

"It's just so great to see you again."

She rolled her eyes.

"We accepted Jesus into our hearts."

"What?"

"At vacation Bible school. Remember? There

was this neat little book we made of construction paper. It didn't have any words in it, but it told a story." His voice brimmed with childlike enthusiasm.

She nodded as the memory returned, and she fought not to smile. Those were good times, when the twins were the dearest of friends. "As I recall, each page was a different color."

"Yes. Now you remember."

"Only vaguely. And I'd like to know what this has to do with you blasting into my life all of a sudden."

"Black for our sins, red for Christ's blood, white for our hearts after Jesus washed them clean," he continued as if she hadn't said a word.

A clean heart? Hardly. Enough was enough, already. "What's your point?"

"In the navy, I'm an RPS."

"What is that, the military's version of a funeral director?"

He chuckled. "Religious Programs Specialist. It's an overglorified name for a secretary."

"You're a *secretary*," Callie repeated, hardly believing her own ears. "There's justice for you."

"You haven't heard the worst of it. I handle the paperwork for the navy chaplains.

"Oh, now there's a good one." She chuckled.

How many times as a child had Colin been the instigator of trouble which Callie usually took the brunt of the blame for? With one major exception—shoplifting.

For a kid who'd been carted off to military school, ending up as a preacher's secretary was truly ironic.

Maybe what came around really did go around. At least in Colin's case.

"What a riot."

"I thought the same thing—for a while. But being around men and women of faith just changes you, somehow. They have this peace about life, even when things go wrong, when there aren't explanations for the bad things that happen."

"I guess you see a lot of bad things in the navy."

He nodded. "Sometimes. Eventually, I started asking questions. I wanted to know what it was that gave their lives so much meaning."

She immediately thought of Rhett, and wondered if she saw the same thing in him as Colin saw in the chaplains. Rhett went to church every weekend, and he talked openly about his faith.

She'd wondered more than once why an otherwise competent man would rely on his faith rather than his own strength. "I think I understand."

"Do you?" Colin smiled eagerly. "It took me a while to realize it wasn't *what* they had, but *Who*."

She frowned. "You lost me."

"Jesus. I rediscovered my relationship with Christ that I lost all those years ago."

"I'm so happy for you."

"I'm serious, Callie."

She met his gaze head-on. "So am I."

"That's why I returned."

"Jesus told you to drive to Oregon and sit on my doorstep?"

"Not in so many words. But when I recommitted myself to God, I realized I had a lot of unresolved issues."

Oh, so now she was an *unresolved issue*. This was getting better and better. "Go home, Colin. You've done your duty before God. You're off the hook."

"It's not like that."

"Whatever. I don't really care."

That wasn't the truth, of course. She cared— too much. But she wouldn't let on. What good would that do? So the new, improved Colin

Brockman would feel better for abandoning his twin sister all those years ago?

She wasn't ready to go that far. Not by a long shot.

"I'm going," Colin said through a stiff jaw. "But not far. I'll be at the Quest Motel at Second and Main. When you're ready, give me a call."

"Don't sit by the phone," she retorted, putting her key into the lock.

"You're the reason I'm here, Callie, and I'm not leaving until we've talked."

"Whatever." Her temples were pounding, and she could think of nothing beyond taking a couple of aspirin and having a good cry.

She stepped through the front door and swung it closed, but even the solid oak of the door didn't keep out Colin's closing remark.

"God bless you, Callie. I'll be praying."

Chapter Eleven

$\backsim\!\!\!\backsim$

When Callie didn't return with his keys, Rhett became concerned. It wasn't that he didn't trust her—quite the opposite, in fact.

She was a woman who kept her word, which was why he became antsy when she didn't show. He wouldn't say he was *worried*, exactly.

Okay, so he *was* worried.

Especially considering the last time he'd seen her was the field house. He could think of all kinds of trouble for her to get into there.

What if one of the boys on parole decided to show up and give her a hard time? What if one of the dogs got loose and she panicked?

He wasn't worried so much about the dogs,

knowing they'd sooner lick her to death than harm her, but he was concerned about Callie's reaction to having the situation out of her control.

He knew her well enough to know she was a control freak. And if she didn't appear confident around the dogs, his less-trained dogs would sense her anxiety and become agitated and unpredictable.

And if one of the big dogs got loose and Callie panicked...

That thought alone was enough to make him grab his car keys, which, thankfully, weren't attached to the field house keys, and drive down to the field house. Just to make sure everything was all right, and Callie was home safe and sound, simply forgetting she'd promised to return them this evening.

He was overreacting, he kept telling himself, but the thought of Callie in any kind of danger drove him on, despite the knowledge of how foolish he'd feel if he were wrong.

He didn't know whether to be relieved or troubled to find that Callie wasn't at the field house. He didn't have the key to get in, but the doors were locked and the safety lights were on.

Apparently, she'd done exactly what she'd said she would do, locked up and gone home.

He chuckled. He was seeing shadows behind every tree these days, and most of them of his own making. So much for the wisdom and maturity of age and faith.

Still smiling, he got on the police radio and asked the dispatcher for Callie's home address, deciding to save her a trip out later. That he was also reassuring his overactive imagination he wouldn't admit—except to himself.

He had to knock twice before she answered.

She peeked out through the one inch of space her chain lock allowed, but even so, Rhett could see that she'd been crying.

"Can I come in?" he asked gently, his concern resurfacing with a vengeance.

Without a word, she closed the door.

He thought that action was the definitive answer to his question until he heard the lock turning, at which point his heart swelled until he could hardly breathe. She reopened the door and gestured him inside.

Her small, ranch-style cottage was typical of the neighborhood. Old and run-down. But he immediately noticed just how much Callie had done with the place to make her house a home.

Frilly gingham curtains hung in the windows,

and there were houseplants galore in every corner of the room.

Not only that, but there was the distinct smell of cinnamon in the air, so alluring it made Rhett's mouth water on the spot.

Arms akimbo, she stared at him for a moment, then shrugged as if in answer to an unspoken question. "I've been baking sugar cookies. Do you want one?"

"You don't have to ask me twice," Rhett agreed, following her into the kitchen. He sat on a bar stool at the end of a breakfast nook while she served him, noting with pleasure the fresh flowers in a vase at the center of the counter.

He wouldn't have pegged Callie as the home-making type. He didn't know exactly what he *had* expected, but somehow he hadn't pictured her buying flowers for herself.

She wasn't the frilly type.

Or was she?

That question was a revelation in itself, and he vowed to learn more about this mysterious entity known as Callie Brockman. It was only in viewing the inside of her house that he realized how much he *didn't* know about her.

And how much he wanted to learn.

She was a tough, independent cop, and he'd

stereotyped her right down to the polyester uniform.

He shook his head. That wouldn't happen again.

"Do you have some milk, by any chance?" he asked, giving her his award-winning smile, the one that had served him well in the past.

Callie didn't appear to notice, never mind be struck down by his charm. "Skim, if that's okay," was her only reply, and that, he thought, was halfhearted.

"Perfect." His grin widened despite her lack of reaction to his previous efforts. "Ever since I was a kid, I've liked to dunk my cookies."

"Me, too." She grimaced in what Rhett guessed was supposed to be a smile, his first hint, besides the red rims of her eyes, that indicated all was not well in Callie's world.

She held up her own half-empty glass of milk, which had been sitting on the counter next to a cookie. "My twin, Colin, and I used to have cookie-dunking races. I guess old habits die hard."

Her bottom lip quivered a moment before her expression turned rigid. Rhett's internal psychologist alarm went off loud and clear. "What's wrong?"

She turned away from him, focusing on taking another batch of cookies out of the oven and placing them, one by one, on some paper towels to cool.

"Callie?"

She threw her spatula onto the counter and grasped the edge with both hands. Staring down at the cookies with a dull glaze over her eyes, she looked very much like someone whose world was spinning out of control.

"There's nothing wrong."

He stood abruptly, his chair nearly tipping underneath him. "Oh, yes there is. I'm a psychologist, remember? Let me help you."

He was surprised at the intensity of his own words. He'd never wanted to help anyone more in his life, except his son.

Perhaps it was *because* of Brandon that Rhett needed to help Callie work out her problems. At least he could help *someone* he cared for.

She remained frozen to the spot, her shoulders shaking with the effort of keeping her emotions restrained.

Years full of helplessness and frustration raged through Rhett, and he sprinted forward, grabbing her by the elbow and twirling her around to face him in a single, fluid motion.

Quickly and deliberately, he slid his hands to her shoulders and gripped her firmly, if tenderly, both amazed and fascinated by how fragile her frame felt beneath his fingers.

The whole of his being reacted to her. Mind. Soul. Body. Spirit.

He wanted to be there for her. With her. He wanted her to know of Jesus, the Rock to which she could cling, and of a mortal man who would be there for her whenever she needed him.

Starting now.

"I can't help you unless you talk to me."

She glared up at him, tears pouring down her cheeks. "You can't help me."

"You don't *know* that."

Before he even realized what he was doing, he'd bent his head, capturing her lips with his own.

He hadn't intended to kiss her, didn't know how or why it had happened; but when she wrapped her arms around his neck, digging her fingers into the hair on the base of his neck and clinging for all she was worth, he deepened the kiss, showing in the best way—the *only* way—he knew how, that she could trust him. That he did care. That he'd be there for her, no matter what.

Words were not enough. Not for the strength and intensity of her emotions. And his.

She wasn't alone.

And neither, he realized, his grip still tight around her, was he.

An audible groan crossed his lips as he wrapped his arms more tightly around her. It seemed like forever since he'd kissed Callie, and it felt good.

Better than good. Phenomenal. Perfect.

With a sudden panicked gasp, she broke off the kiss and slapped her hand over her mouth, as if horrified at what they'd done.

He dropped his arms at once. An apology hovered on his lips, but as he made to move away, she turned and stepped back into his embrace, burying her head on his shoulder and wrapping her arms tightly around his waist, as if he were her only anchor amidst a violent storm.

Sighing, he pulled her close, inhaling the soft, musky smell that was Callie. He brushed stray wisps of her silky, silver hair away from her temple with his fingertips, mumbling softly all the while, giving her everything he possessed, words of peace and strength.

As for himself, he was content with the moment.

For once in his life, the first time in more years than he cared to count, he really believed things were going to be all right. And he wanted more than anything to share that divine assurance with Callie, who was groping in the dark for a beacon, for *Light*.

To think they might have missed each other, and all because of his stubborn pride, his unwillingness to listen and his ridiculous ideas of what his future wife should be.

He now recognized his version of perfection was so far from what he *needed* that it wasn't even funny.

Or maybe funny was exactly what it was.

God knew all along. Thank God He knew.

"My twin brother came here today," she murmured, her whisper muffled by his button-down cotton shirt. "I haven't seen him in years."

Callie had mentioned she was a twin in several of their conversations together, but Rhett couldn't remember any specifics.

Even a name eluded him, which surprised him, as he was usually good at remembering names. He searched the depths of his mind, but still came up empty. "Your twin?"

"Colin."

"I take it this wasn't a planned visit."

She laughed bitterly. "It's been over 10 years. I didn't even know where to find him."

He frowned, but remained silent. She looked as if she carried the burden of the world on her slim, squared shoulders, and he wished he could carry some of the load for her, even if it were only for a moment.

"My father sent him off to military school after he got into trouble with the law. He was only sixteen—Brandon's age."

Suddenly, the whole outrageous history between them, all the times she'd spoken on Brandon's behalf, made perfect sense.

She'd already walked this road. Why hadn't he seen this earlier?

She hiccupped, and Rhett pulled a tissue from a box on the counter and handed it to her with a gentle smile. "Go on."

The least he could do now was listen. He only wished he could do more. And maybe he could, if given the right information and half a chance.

"Colin hated military school with a passion. And he hated my father for sending him there in the first place. Maybe he hated me, too, for not standing up to Dad when I should have. The whole stupid shoplifting scheme was my idea. I'm sure he thought of that often when he was put through his military paces and sculpted into something he was not.''

"No," Rhett denied immediately.

No brother could hate Callie, especially a twin. No matter what she'd thought she'd done, what role she'd played in this farce.

He wouldn't believe that of Colin, though he'd never met the man. What little Callie had spoken about her brother had been in love. Twins, in Rhett's vast experience as a counselor, shared many of the same traits.

He thought he might like to meet this Colin.

Her brother would no doubt enlighten Rhett on many facets of Callie's personality he was eager to unearth.

"My father was so bitter, he wouldn't even attend Colin's graduation. He was miserable after my mother died, and he took it out on Colin.

"I was too frightened of my own shadow to go against my father's wishes and attend Colin's graduation, and I've regretted that decision every day of my life. I should have been there. He expected it of me."

Her thoughts had turned inward, and it showed in the anger of her tone. "I betrayed him, and I've paid for it over and over again."

Rhett didn't think what happened between the

twins was Callie's fault, nor did he think her twin was blaming her for half the guilt she pinned on herself.

But she wasn't ready to hear his professional opinion on the matter, so he asked a question instead.

"What happened to Colin?"

"He disappeared." She looked out the kitchen window into the darkness, the gleam of tears in her eyes making them glitter like precious metal.

"I tried to find him, but I couldn't afford a private investigator, and Colin didn't want to be found."

A lone tear slid down her cheek, and Rhett wiped it away with his fingertip.

"I've lived with that guilt ever since. It's been eleven years." She shook her head. "Eleven long, silent years with not a word from him.

"I knew he was alive, because we share a special, unexplainable bond with each other. You know—feeling each other's pain and happiness? But I couldn't find him."

Pain laced her voice, and her words explained a lot, like why she'd become a juvenile police officer, and why she was so passionate about her work.

And why she cared so much about what happened between Rhett and Brandon.

"But he showed up today." It was a statement, and she nodded.

"Where has he been all this time?"

She made a sound in her throat that was half a laugh, half a snort. "Would you believe he joined the navy?"

"I thought he hated military school."

"He did. That's what's so laughable." She didn't sound like she wanted to laugh.

"He's a career navy man?"

"Yeah. Go figure."

"Did he say why he's suddenly decided to renew family ties?"

"Oh, that's the real kicker. *God* told him to come to Oregon and find me."

"God *told* him to come?" Rhett's voice revealed the skepticism he felt.

"Well, not audibly or anything," she admitted, waving him off. "But what difference does it make? He really believes God sent him here. All I know is, God didn't mention it to me."

"Didn't He?" Rhett's heart leapt. He could feel her spiritual dilemma as if it were his own, and he remembered being in the same quandary of faith at one time.

Callie's eyebrows bunched into a V over her nose. "Give me a break. God doesn't talk to me."

"Is that a fact?"

"That's a fact," she repeated angrily. "Let's just say I'm not on God's list of good graces."

He didn't know about that.

Callie was running, and God was chasing. If he wasn't mistaken, her heels were being divinely nipped and she was panicking.

He knew the feeling well.

"Did your brother say anything specific, besides that God sent him?"

Callie shook her head. "I showed him the door. I was very upset, and not ready to deal with Colin yet. He caught me off guard."

She shook her head again, more fervently this time, and picked up her half-eaten cookie. "I bake when I need to think."

"Good thing for me," he quipped lightly, hoisting his own cookie in a salute.

"You're welcome to the whole batch of them. My hips sure don't need any encouragement."

Her hips were just perfect in Rhett's view, but he thought it expedient not to comment.

"I don't know what Colin *really* wanted, but whatever it was, he isn't through with me yet. He told me he's staying at the Quest Motel. He seemed to be under the impression I'd be contacting him soon."

"Won't you?"

She chuckled, for real this time. "I suppose. Once I get my bearings, anyway."

"Sounds to me like he might be here to ask your forgiveness."

"*My* forgiveness? I'm the one who needs to ask forgiveness. Colin didn't do anything wrong."

"Yet you're angry with him."

Callie blew out a breath. "Of course I'm angry. He could have let me know where he was. Or that he was okay, at least."

"Then you *do* need to forgive him."

"Forgive and forget," she quipped, frowning. "I don't think I'll ever forget what he put me through."

"God's not asking you to forget, Callie. But He does want you to forgive your brother."

"It hurts too much."

Rhett nodded, remembering how difficult it was to forgive Kayla after she'd left him and their marriage. There was nothing harder in the world, and he felt for Callie, being faced with what she considered her brother's betrayal.

"Forgiveness is a choice," he said slowly, softly, knowing his words wouldn't be easy for her to hear, much less come to grips with. "Not a feeling. A choice."

Her brows hit her hairline. "What's that supposed to mean?"

"It means you can forgive Colin even if you don't *feel* forgiveness in your heart."

"What? I just wave my wand around and say the magic words?"

Rhett chuckled and shook his head. "I wish it was that easy, but it isn't. Forgiving Colin—and your father—will be one of the toughest things you'll ever do."

"Leave my father out of this," she snapped.

He held up his hands, palms out. "Okay. Let's just deal with Colin right now."

Rhett didn't want to ruffle Callie's feathers. He wanted to soothe her, to take away her pain. Yet he was compelled to continue, knowing his words weren't what Callie wanted to hear.

"Unforgiveness is like a cancer. It eats away at you, and it's every bit as terminal as any disease. The best thing you can do for *yourself* right now is to meet with your brother and initiate forgiveness. For both of you."

"So then, let me see if I've got this straight. I just have to say I forgive Colin to his face, even though I don't feel that way." To say she sounded

unconvinced would have been an understatement.
"And that's it?"

"No. There's more."

"Now, why am I not surprised?"

"Then," he continued, ignoring her cutting remark, "you have to act out your forgiveness. Put
it all behind you and start over. Don't you want
to have a relationship with your brother?"

"I don't know what I want." She popped another cookie into her mouth, chewed slowly, and
swallowed. "I love my brother, but I'm too angry
to even think about forgiving him right now."

"As well you should be. No one is discounting
your anger."

"Not even God?"

"Especially not God. 'Be angry and sin not,'
are His words, not mine."

"I'll think about it."

"Pray?" He knew he was pushing it, but his
tongue got the better of him.

"Think," she assured him.

"Good enough," he conceded, knowing he'd
planted a seed. She'd be thinking about her faith,
even if she wouldn't call what she was doing
praying.

God was doing something special here, and
Rhett was blessed to be a part of it. Somehow,

some way, God was going to make lemonade out of lemons.

And Rhett couldn't wait to taste the finished product.

Chapter Twelve

Callie picked up the telephone receiver again, but just as she'd done the other hundred times she'd picked it up and put it to her ear, she sighed and put it back in its cradle without dialing.

She'd never expected that seeing her brother again would be so painful, no matter how angry she was with him. No matter what was between them.

They were *twins*.

They'd been best friends as children, inseparable even as teenagers. Colin knew everything about her. They'd often thought or said the same thing at the same time, then laughed over the coincidence.

Everything was wonderful between them until Colin stole something from the five-and-dime on a dare, and had been caught in the act by the store's angry owner. It was his first offense, but the owner didn't care, and prosecuted Colin for that stupid stunt.

That one moment had changed both their lives.

She'd give anything to go back to that day, before it all happened, to beg him to stop before he started, instead of egging him on as she'd done.

In a very real sense, his crime was hers. She was the mastermind behind the plan, and she'd been the big mouth who'd made the dare Colin couldn't do anything else but accept.

The crime was hers. In every way but the way that counted. *She* hadn't been carted off to the police station. *She* hadn't been the one on the receiving end of Dad's solemn silence, so much worse than anything he said aloud. And *she* hadn't been the one sent away to military boarding school.

No, but she wished she had. *She'd* been the one left behind. And she'd regretted it with every breath since the day it happened, even if her own teenage years weren't much better than Colin's had been. How many times had she wished *she'd* been the one who was sent far away from her gruff and untouchable father?

But what was done, was done. There was no sense dredging up the past. If wishes were horses...or days...

Yet how could she ignore the past, with it staring her in the face; a living, breathing past who'd grown from a boy into a man?

And she had grown up, as well.

Should she do as Rhett suggested, and put the past to rest? Could she start new with Colin, attempt to regain the close relationship they'd once so easily shared?

But she didn't know him at all, and it frightened her. He'd been a gawky teenager the last time she'd seen him, and she'd been a painfully shy, zit-covered tenth grader.

How could they pick up where they left off? Their lives had taken such different paths. She didn't know if they had the slightest thing in common anymore, other than their birthdays and the color of their hair.

She'd spent the night tossing and turning, her mind going over Colin's abrupt arrival into her life.

Every word they'd said to each other. Every tingle of emotion she experienced.

What should she do?

She wasn't ready to face Colin. Not a morning person on the best of days, she was definitely the worse for wear from her sleepless night. She didn't think even a fully caffeinated double shot of espresso could repair the damage.

She wondered what Rhett was doing. Sleeping, if he had any sense.

He'd stayed late, casually hovering around until he was certain she'd be okay. And not for the first time, she was glad he'd been there for her. She was thankful fate—or *God,* as Rhett would say—had arranged the circumstances so he had come for his keys last night.

She should be annoyed, but she wasn't. *Grateful* was more along the lines of her feelings for Rhett right now.

Gratefulness, and something more.

She didn't know *how* to classify Rhett's kisses, or her reaction. His lips had met hers as a challenge, yet had quickly turned into something else; a different, deeper kind of challenge.

And she'd picked up the gauntlet before she had a chance to give it a rational thought.

Though he wasn't the first man she'd ever kissed, Rhett was the first man ever to affect her heart as well as her body; making her lose all sense of time and place, aware of nothing but the warmth of the ever growing ember between them.

Even *thinking* about Rhett made her weak in the knees, which was only marginally preferable to the quandary she felt when she thought of Colin.

Since it was Saturday morning and she had the day off, she pulled on an old pair of sweats, deciding she'd distract herself with a pile of rented videotapes—romantic comedies without a hint of reality in them. Not a drama or tearjerker among them.

She'd seen enough reality to last her a good long while.

Rhett mopped the perspiration off his brow with a handkerchief. Though the day was crisp and cool, he was sweating up a storm, and it wasn't from physical exertion.

Brandon was gone.

He knew something serious had been eating at his son. The fist-size hole in his office wall was proof of that. And his trouble with the law was another bright beacon in the dark night of the teenage soul.

But to run away?

Maybe he was wrong. He prayed he was mistaken. Brandon's drawers had been shuffled through and left open. Clothes had been yanked from hangers. Most telling of all, the game-winning football from his first touchdown as a running back on the Grant Union Prospectors varsity team was conspicuously missing from the center of his top bookshelf.

Rhett wanted to yell with rage and frustration. It was his fault. He'd been laboring under the mis-apprehension things between them were getting better, but he was obviously mistaken. He'd either genuinely misread the signs Brandon was display-ing, or he was the singularly most clueless indi-vidual who'd ever roamed the planet.

At the moment, he was inclined to believe the latter.

What was going on with his son that he didn't know about? Why wasn't Brandon talking to him? Hadn't their prayer time together meant any-thing?

He'd been so sure, so encouraged by the prog-ress they were making together, with God's help.

They were beginning to rebuild their relation-ship, the close father-son bond they'd once shared. Finally, they were moving past the prob-lem and into solutions.

And now this.

He was leveled by the unwanted, unexpected revelation. It felt like a slap on the face.

What was he supposed to do now? What was Brandon really after? What did he want Rhett to do?

And why did he feel the need to lash out in yet another drastic, attention-getting tactic?

If that's what it was. Rhett wasn't sure of anything, anymore.

"Oh, Lord God, protect my son," he murmured, scrubbing his fingers across his scalp where a headache was forming. He breathed heavily, willing his blood to stop pounding and roaring through his head.

His heart throbbed an erratic tattoo to the beat of his guilty conscience.

All my fault. All my fault.

There wasn't anyone else here to blame. Without a woman's—a *mother's*—guidance, and with his father making only flailing attempts at parenthood, the boy was left to his own devices.

No need to mince words in his mind. If Brandon was gone, it was completely Rhett's fault.

Some dad he turned out to be.

If he felt any anxiety as an eighteen-year-old with a wife and infant son, he was under twice as much pressure now. And while there were books galore on baby care, he hadn't run across many handbooks on the care and feeding of a teenager.

He'd laugh, if he wasn't so close to tears.

When he'd arrived home after staying late at Callie's, Brandon had been sound asleep in his room, though how he could sleep with his stereo blaring loud enough to shake the walls, Rhett would never know.

Brandon didn't even twitch when Rhett brushed the hair off the boy's forehead and planted a tender, fatherly kiss on his temple.

What could have happened between last night and this morning that had set Brandon off? He hadn't heard the phone ring, nor the doorbell peal.

No matter. Either way, the boy was gone.

Rhett immediately called down to the station to request a special favor—a private investigator who'd know what to look for, where to find clues that would help them find the boy.

All this done *off* the record, of course. He knew he couldn't file a missing persons report for another day, and even then, he wasn't sure what good that would serve.

Unfortunately, it was a busy Saturday for the precinct, and every officer there was on active duty. No chance for a little off-the-record help today.

Rhett paced back and forth through his son's room, jamming his fingers through his hair. Pounding his fist into his opposite palm. Trying to think things through when his brain felt muddled and his head was hammering with apprehension and anxiety.

Suddenly it came to him out of nowhere. Not the answer to his problem, but maybe the next best thing.

There was someone else he could call for help. He reached for Brandon's telephone.

When he found his son, things would be different. He'd pay attention to the things that Brandon was interested in, things that mattered to the boy, instead of always being so caught up in his work.

He wondered how much *more* he didn't know about his son. What else went on in Brandon's life that he didn't know about?

No wonder the kid was running.

Rhett hesitated a moment more, then set his jaw and dialed the number he'd committed to memory, though he'd never had a reason to call.

"Callie?" he bit out from between clenched jaws when she answered. "Can you come to my house?"

"Sure," she agreed amicably. "Should I bring lunch?"

"No. No lunch," he rasped.

"Rhett, what's wrong?" Worry edged her voice.

"It's nothing." *It's everything. Oh, dear Lord, Brandon is gone.* "Brandon is gone."

"What do you mean Brandon is gone? *Gone* gone?" She sounded as frantic as he felt.

"Yeah," he agreed softly. "I think so. As far as I can tell. Some of his clothes are missing, and I can't find his duffel bag." He knew he sounded like a frog with a head cold, but he didn't care.

"I'll be right over," she said hastily, just before the dial tone buzzed in his ear.

Rhett couldn't believe the relief that flooded his chest. Callie would be here soon.

Not knowing what else to do, he slumped to his knees by the side of Brandon's bed and clenched his hands together.

"Oh, God." It was in every way a prayer, though he lost his voice when he tried to go further. He bowed his head, spending an indefinite moment silently reaching for the comfort and solace of heavenly arms.

Oh, how his heart ached. God knew where

Brandon was, and He was the *only* one who knew. "Please don't take Brandon away from me."

It was the prayer of a broken man.

"God wouldn't do that."

Callie's soft words made him jolt to his feet. He hadn't realized he was praying aloud, never mind that anyone other than God was listening.

Heat rushed to his face. He cleared his throat and jammed his hands into the front pockets of his jeans.

Without another word, Callie wrapped her arms around him and buried her face in his shoulder. Rhett stiffened, then bowed his head into the silky softness of her hair and clung to her like a lifeline.

After several minutes, she stepped back. Tears streamed from her eyes, wetting her cheeks with dark traces of mascara. In Rhett's estimation, she'd never looked lovelier.

"What should I do?" he asked, trying desperately to still the frantic hammering of his heart and keep his voice calm and even.

He failed miserably at both.

"Where have you searched?" Relief surged through him, acting as a buffer for all these unfamiliar, polar emotions he was experiencing.

Callie was here. She'd help him think things

through in a calm, rational manner. Her mere presence made a tremendous difference.

He didn't have to face this alone.

He cleared his throat, trying to focus. "First thing after I knew he was gone, I phoned the pizza parlor, and the pool hall. He hangs out there a lot with other kids his age."

He paused and swept in a breath that stung his lungs as if it were carbon dioxide and not fresh oxygen. "I called everywhere I could think of where he might have gone."

"I even called his girlfriend," he concluded with a bitter laugh.

"That's a reasonable course of action," she assured him. "You've done the right thing, Rhett."

He wasn't sure if she referred to calling the pool hall or calling her, but it didn't make any difference.

"It doesn't feel reasonable," he snapped harshly, but Callie didn't exhibit any reaction. In fact, she didn't move a muscle.

"I *feel* like calling the precinct and putting out an all-points bulletin. But I can't even register Brandon as missing for another nineteen and a half hours."

Callie smiled sadly. "Not that you're counting."

He pursed his lips, fighting the new wave of dread washing over him. "I'm probably overreacting."

"Rhett, you're a wonderful father."

"Yeah, that's why my kid has run off."

He couldn't take it anymore. He slammed his fist into the door frame, making a small dent in the trim and a large gash on his hand. And the worst part was, it didn't hold a candle to the pain in his heart.

"You aren't going to help Brandon by hurting yourself," Callie reproved, though her voice was gentle.

She pulled a handkerchief from her purse and wrapped it around Rhett's bloody knuckles. Even through his panic, he appreciated the tender gesture.

"Are you absolutely positive he's run away? I mean, maybe he just needed a little space or something. Could he be walking around the block?"

He made a strangled sound in his throat and turned away, but Callie grabbed his elbow and turned him around.

"It's early yet," she said firmly, forcing his gaze to lock with hers, allowing encouragement to flow from her heart to his. "This might not be as bad as you think."

He shrugged. "I guess not."

Suddenly, she snapped her fingers and her face brightened considerably. "Hey, I know! Did you try the church?"

He frowned. "No. Why? Do you think he might have gone there? It's Saturday. I didn't even think about church."

"Maybe you should have." Callie flashed him a confident, secretive smile. "The church has one very important item you don't have. And I'm relatively certain he won't find that item at the pizza parlor or pool hall, either."

"What would that be?"

"A punching bag."

She grabbed for his hand and dragged him at a trot out of Brandon's room and down the stairs to the main entrance, excitement adding bounce to her step.

"I have a hunch, Rhett."

He had no answer to that, so he numbly followed her out to her car. It didn't even occur to him to offer to drive until they were halfway to the church, with Callie in the driver's seat.

"I was just thinking about the last time I was

at the church. We were in the gym, remember?"
Callie asked softly, breaking the silence.

Rhett stared forward, his jaw locked and his
head throbbing.

"If I recall, we weren't on the best of terms."
She reached across the seat and took his hand.

"No," he agreed quietly.

She shifted her gaze to him, then back to the
road. "I'm glad we're friends, Rhett."

"Me, too, Callie," he said, interlacing their fingers and squeezing her hand gently. *Friend* didn't
even begin to describe his feelings for Callie and
he struggled to find words to express all she'd
become to him. "I don't know what I'd do without you."

They pulled into the church parking lot and
Rhett tensed to the point of physical pain. He was
afraid even to hope Callie's hunch was right, and
yet…

"Well, you don't have to worry about what
you'd do without me, because I'll be there whenever you need me, whether you like it or not."
She squeezed his hand again.

"You're not alone. I'm here with you now, and
we're going to find Brandon. Everything's going
to be all right."

Callie hoped she was right.

"*God* is with Brandon," she added for good measure. "You trust God to take care of him, don't you?"

Rhett looked confused for a moment, then nodded. "God." He buried his face in his hands and his shoulders shook with the intensity of keeping his feelings under wraps.

Callie put her arm around his shoulders, encouraging him the only way she knew, as words deserted her.

If there was a God, He *had* to be listening to Rhett right now. The poor man had paid a lifetime of penance in the past half hour.

He was a good man. He didn't deserve this. He'd tried his best to raise Brandon.

Why was God punishing him this way? She directed her anger heavenward and practically dared God to send a bolt of lightning to strike her for her horrible, sacrilegious thoughts.

Better to blame God than Rhett.

She brushed aside the parallel thought that she'd once been just as judgmental about Rhett's parenting abilities as he was now being of himself.

She knew better now.

And if she knew, God knew. She had to believe that.

Rhett had to believe that. He needed a divine lifeline right about now. Callie silently prayed—*really* prayed—for the first time in years.

And then, summoning up every last bit of courage she possessed, she exited the car and waited for Rhett to do the same.

Chapter Thirteen

Rhett's first glimpse of his son was when he rushed around the corner of the door to the church gym. Brandon was giving the punching bag a series of short *one-two* bursts, sweat and what Rhett thought were tears streaming down his face.

Relief flooded through him so powerfully it almost buckled his knees. All at once, he was berating himself for overreacting, and thanking God that Brandon was safe and still in John Day.

All the bad things Rhett had imagined were swept from him by emotion so great he could barely contain it. Anger and elation warred for prominence within his heart, and he took deep, gulping breaths of air to calm himself.

Brandon's duffel bag was lying haphazardly on the floor next to him, the contents pouring out. Sweats, a T-shirt, shoulder pads, and the football that belonged in the middle of Brandon's shelf.

All present and accounted for.

Rhett felt a sharp nudge that jolted him from his stupor. He looked down and realized it was Callie's elbow jabbing into his ribs.

"Go to him," she said softly, gesturing her head in Brandon's direction.

He reached for her hand, but she pulled away. "No. This is between you and Brandon. I don't want to interfere."

He knew her words were right and true. He was a psychologist, after all, for all the good it did him. He knew the textbook theories of reuniting families.

But even so, he needed the security of her hand in his, and dreaded facing his son alone.

What could he possibly say to make things right?

"Brandon." The word came out as a toad's croak, so he tried again. "Brandon."

"Dad!" Brandon stepped away from the punching bag and gazed wide-eyed as Rhett approached. "I didn't expect to see you here today."

"I didn't expect to see you, either," Rhett replied, feeling as if he were choking on his words. "You were gone this morning when I woke up."

"I wanted to get an early start," Brandon commented, then punched the bag *one-two.*

"An early start? At what?"

That question sent Brandon into a series of punches, and he looked as if he were fighting back tears, even through the sweat. His eyes were red rimmed and his jaw was clenched.

"I was worried about you, son."

Brandon stopped punching and wiped the sweat off his forehead with his arm. "Why?"

Rhett didn't know whether to laugh or cry. "I thought you might have run away."

It was only now that he realized *why* he'd panicked so completely when he thought Brandon had taken off on him.

Kayla.

She'd left him in the middle of the day, while he was at work. No Dear John letter. No clues explaining why she left. Just ruffled drawers, hangers all askew, and—

His stomach clenched so tightly he thought he might wretch.

The snow-globe.

She'd taken *The Phantom of the Opera* snow-globe from their mantel when she left. The expensive mask-and-rose keepsake he'd surprised her with on their first Christmas together was gone, along with his wife of eight years.

The memory drifted back, clouded and buffered by time. Kayla was a Broadway aficionado. They'd even flown to New York for a weekend one summer.

And that's how he knew for sure she was gone for good.

The snow-globe represented their marriage, in a way, though he hadn't recognized that fact until now. When he'd seen the conspicuously empty mantel, he'd broken down and cried.

And ever since that day eight years ago, he'd been paying for it with every breath he took and every beat of his heart.

They'd eventually worked out their problems, Kayla and he. And then on the verge of Kayla's return home, she'd caught meningitis and died within the week, leaving Rhett alone with an eight-year-old son to raise.

And *that* was why seeing Brandon's football missing had sent out an all-points bulletin in his mind. It was just a little too familiar for comfort.

Brandon hadn't replied to Rhett's statement,

other than to continue punching the bag with re-
newed enthusiasm.

"Can you stop swinging for just a moment?"
Rhett snapped, his fear now exhibiting as anger.

"Yeah, sure." He obeyed, but he looked sullen
in complying.

"Why did you take your football with you?"

It was all he could think of to say, and he was
stuttering the words through a dry throat as it was.

But he had to know.

Brandon shook his head. "I don't want to talk
about it."

Without thinking, Rhett stomped forward and
swung his son around by the elbow. "Well,
you're *going* to talk about it, young man."

Aaauuugh. Exactly the wrong thing to say, and
especially the wrong way to say it. After all this
worrying, he came down hard on Brandon? Whoever said *old habits die hard* wasn't kidding.

"I'm sorry," father and son said in unison,
then laughed.

"You go first." Again, they'd spoken in perfect unison.

"I came here looking for you," Rhett said, affectionately socking his son on his shoulder.

"Me? Why?"

"I think you can answer that question," he replied.

Brandon's face paled. "You thought I ran off."

Rhett could only nod, for the lump in his throat had grown to bowling ball proportions.

His son's dark eyebrows scrunched over his blue eyes. "I wouldn't do that. I'm not like—" He shut his mouth abruptly when he realized what he was going to say.

"No, you're not like your mother," Rhett assured him. "At least, not in that way." He ruffled his son's hair. "You do have her eyes."

"I'm not going anywhere, Dad," Brandon affirmed, his voice hoarse and cracking. "I swear it."

"I'm glad to hear that." Now it was Rhett's voice that was cracking, sounding every bit as awkward as his gangly teenage boy's.

"Dad?" Brandon sounded concerned.

Rhett squeezed his eyes shut for a moment and took a deep breath, regaining his control.

"Tell me," he said, pinching the top of his nose against a sudden headache, "why you took your football with you this morning."

Brandon swung a sudden left, square on. The punching bag swung wildly. "I don't want to tell you."

"Why not?"

Brandon answered with a *left-right-left*. "Because it's stupid."

Rhett reminded himself to keep it cool, composed. "Tell me anyway? When you're ready to talk, I mean."

Brandon's gaze switched to the door. "You can come in, Miss Brockman," he said, cracking his serious veneer.

Rhett's face warmed. "How did you know?"

"Are you kidding?" *Left-right-left*. "You smell like her."

"Better than I usually smell, huh?"

Brandon chuckled. "Yeah. Much better."

Callie laughed as she exposed herself from her hiding place. "I'm afraid I'm just as guilty as your father. Vanilla Musk. I never leave home without it."

"Yeah, but how come *I* smell like Vanilla Musk?" he asked, rubbing the back of his neck, kneading his pinched muscles.

The movement did, in fact, send a whiff of her delicious-smelling perfume through his senses.

"I always put a dab of perfume on my wrist in the morning," she admitted.

Now why did her wide grin remind Rhett of the Cheshire cat's craftiness?

"It must have rubbed off when you were holding my hand."

The cinders already scorching on Rhett's face turned into a bonfire and he didn't dare look at his son. What must Brandon think?

"Should I get out of here and leave the two of you alone?" This from his obviously incorrigible son's mouth, and Rhett's gaze immediately ping-ponged between Brandon and Callie.

Their expressions were identical—a conniving blend of indulgence and amusement. It looked suspiciously as if they were collaborating.

Rhett crossed his arms over his chest and huffed. The brunt of a joke, when only moments before he'd been in a heart-wrenching situation.

The two in question laughed out loud at his harebrained reaction to their teasing.

His gaze switched to Callie, and he belatedly realized what she'd done. With one smile, she had turned a tension-wrought situation *he'd* created into circumstances they could all smile and joke about.

For the first time since he'd discovered Brandon missing that morning, he smiled as well.

Thank you, Jesus!

Callie definitely deserved his thanks, as well. It was a team effort, if he'd ever seen one.

"You want to show me how to throw this thing?" Callie asked Brandon, hefting his prize-winning football.

"He can teach you how to be a linebacker," Rhett teased. "But a quarterback he's not."

"Linebacker? That sounds daunting."

"Nah. You can do it. Go out for a pass." Brandon popped the ball from Callie's grasp and ran backward, hefting the ball with one arm. "Not a quarterback, huh, Dad?"

"The only kind of *going out* I know about involves dinner and a movie." Callie laughed and waggled her eyebrows.

"He means run that way," Rhett said, pointing to the far wall.

"Okay, if you say so." Callie took off at a jog.

"I suggest you look back from time to time," Rhett coached, "or Brandon's liable to zing you in the back of your head."

"Dad. I'm not *that* bad."

"Just warning her."

"What am I supposed to do now?" Callie called from the other side of the gym.

Rhett chuckled. "Look heavenward and pray."

Both Brandon and Callie proved him wrong in an instant, and his jaw dropped in amazement.

Not only did Brandon spiral the football right

into her arms, but Callie *caught* it, and didn't even bother to make it look difficult.

Her arms in a victory *V*, she trotted back to where Rhett and Brandon were standing, wide-eyed. "Yeah! And the crowd goes wild!"

Rhett narrowed his eyes on her, his suspicion growing. "Dinner and a movie, huh?"

Callie shrugged and bent over the football. "Blue Thirty-Two," she called to her left. "Blue Thirty-Two," she called to her right. "Hut, hut."

She pulled the ball shoulder high and faked a pass. "Okay, Shrink, go long."

She didn't have to tell him twice. Rhett tossed a glance behind him and ran for the opposite end of the gym, his tennis shoes squeaking on the polished wood floor.

"Hey, Brandon, are you going to blitz her or not?" he called, but a moment later the football hit him square in the chest—a throw any dolt could catch, much less a man who was once a high school halfback.

As he returned the ball, the light, silvery peal of Callie's laughter rang in his ears.

"Where did I go wrong?" he asked, grinning like an ape with a bushel of bananas.

"You forgot I have a twin brother," she said, playfully socking him on the shoulder. "Colin didn't go for dolls, so I learned how to play football.''

"Cool," Brandon said, knocking the football from his father and tossing it in the air.

"Smear, to be exact."

"Smear?" asked Rhett and Brandon simultaneously.

Callie flushed. "I'm showing my age here, aren't I?

"Too old for you," she said ruffling Brandon's hair. "And too young for you." She winked at Rhett.

"Hey, now," he warned. "Watch the cheap shots. What are the rules for this Smear I'm too old to play?" he teased. "It sounds promising to me."

"Trust me, you're too old," she said, her eyes sparkling. *"I'm* too old. I'm definitely not suggesting it as a family game."

Her cheeks flamed attractively, and she rushed on, covering her faux pas with more words. "Smear is a game for the *very* young—those that don't mind getting their brains bashed in."

"That's my son," Rhett said, slapping Brandon on the back. "He goes out of his way to find opportunities for him to get his brains bashed in."

"Dad," Brandon warned. And to Callie, "Can you show me how to play?"

Callie barked out a laugh. "No, I won't show you. But I'll tell you about it, if you're that interested."

"Humor us," Rhett entreated.

"Okay. Well, the guy—or girl—with the football spirals it straight into the air. Then whoever catches the ball dodges around trying to get away from everyone else."

She smiled widely. "Who are, of course, all aiming to tackle the one with the ball."

Rhett lifted his eyebrows. "That's it?"

Callie nodded emphatically. "That's it. I told you it was for young people who wanted their brains bashed in. No reasonable, mature adult would play Smear."

Brandon laughed aloud, then tossed the ball in the air and called, "Smear!"

"The really scary thing," Callie continued, ignoring the football that bounced off her shoulder, "is that Colin used to talk me into *catching* the ball when we played that game as kids. Is that lame or what?"

"Sounds pretty gutsy to me," said Rhett.

"Stupid, not gutsy," Callie corrected. "Which is, perhaps, why my present circumstances compel me to carry a gun and get my brains bashed in on a regular basis. Those young-girl brain cells that were supposed to protect me from such idiocy obviously got knocked out of me playing Smear."

She flashed both of them a feisty grin, her silver-blue eyes sparkling with mirth. "Hmm. I wonder what that says about male brain cells, since little *boys* usually…"

She let the sentence dangle.

Rhett wrapped his arms around her tiny waist and swung her around, tickling her ribs.

She screeched in protest.

"Don't go there, lady," he warned with a low, playful growl.

"So, hey," Brandon interrupted. "Are we going to play football, or what?"

Callie reached for the ball. "As long as it's not Smear, you're on."

Rhett grinned wickedly. "Boys against girls?"

Her laugh was light and silvery, as was the gleam in her eyes. "Of course," she said, tucking the football under her arm. "What else?"

Chapter Fourteen

"So anyway, since I've been forbidden to go out for football this year," explained Brandon as he swept out the gym, "I decided to see if I could form a team at church."

Callie was impressed. Football was obviously a big part of Brandon's life. He didn't make the statement with any kind of malice, but rather with a remarkable maturity that showed he could swallow the pills life offered, accepting the bitter with the good.

"And?" Rhett asked, looking up from where he was mopping the floor.

Callie's throat swelled with emotion as she witnessed the love and compassion shining like a beacon from Rhett's eyes.

It was that look, more than the feel of his arms around her waist earlier—as nice as that had been—that made her heart soar. She wanted to throw her arms around his neck and never let go.

Fortunately for both the Wheeler men, she restrained herself admirably.

"Did the other kids leave before we got here?" Callie asked, remembering the train of conversation and Rhett's unanswered question.

"They never showed."

Brandon murmured the words under his breath, and Callie thought Rhett probably didn't hear his answer.

"No one?" she asked gently, quietly, instinctively certain Brandon didn't want his father to know.

"No one," Brandon confirmed, looking away.

"Oh, now, you can't say that," she admonished loudly, bringing Rhett into the picture without exposing Brandon's inner heart for public display. "Your old man and I play a mean game of football."

Brandon smiled, the same adorable, lopsided grin that made his father so attractive. "Yeah, I guess you're right. No big deal."

"I'm glad to hear it," Rhett said, misinterpreting the words.

Callie didn't try to enlighten him. "Are you big, sweaty fellows ready to get some chow, or am I the only one with a rumbly in my tumbly?"

Rhett laid an arm across her shoulders and guided her toward the door. He was drenched with sweat, she hadn't been kidding about that. But she wasn't about to squawk about the steamy, appealing mix of aftershave, sweat and man. He was all male, and she was enjoying every moment in his arms.

It was only now, playing football with Rhett and his son, that she realized why her heart zinged every time she saw—or even thought about— Rhett Wheeler. Smiling, she kept her newfound knowledge to herself.

"Pooh Bear, in case you were wondering about the reference," she said instead, patting her stomach.

"I knew that," Rhett insisted. "What, do you think I had a deprived childhood or something?"

She didn't want to shrug, afraid he'd remove his arm from her shoulders, so she just cocked her head so she could smell the fresh wintergreen of his breath. "I wouldn't say *deprived,* exactly. It's just that all that football…"

"She's got you there, Dad," Brandon chimed

in. "I think we ought to go out for pizza. What do you say, Callie?"

Callie exchanged glances with Rhett to see his reaction. He smiled and nodded.

"Anything but those disgusting little fishy-things," she agreed happily.

Rhett snapped his fingers and shook his head. "And here Brandon and I were looking forward to our usual—double anchovies with extra fish—I mean, cheese."

Since she and Rhett had arrived in her SUV, she handed him the keys and motioned Brandon into the back seat.

"You put so much as a scratch on this truck and you won't like what's coming to you, Wheeler," she teased. "No mercy."

He threw his hands up in protest. "Hey. I'm an excellent driver."

"I'll drive," Brandon offered.

"No," both adults said simultaneously.

"Sheesh, I was only asking."

"Ask with somebody else's vehicle, kiddo," Callie said, shaking her finger at him in rebuke. "Buck here is my pride and joy."

"Buck?" asked Rhett, his voice a combination of disbelief and amusement.

"Buck the Wonder Truck." She gave him her

best Southern belle smile. "What, you big, handsome, muscle-bound men don't name your cars?" She swatted him with a fan made of her spread fingers. "Now, Rhett!"

He grinned. "Frankly, my dear—" he paused and flashed her his crooked grin. "Men do *not* name their vehicles."

"Well, women do." She paused and scrunched her eyebrows together. "At least, I do."

"Must be all those extra brain cells," Brandon commented from the back seat.

"Keep it up, kiddo, and you're going to get anchovies for dinner, hold the pizza." Callie shot him her best scowl.

They pulled into the pizza joint, and Brandon was out the door without a word.

"We won't see him until the pizza arrives," Rhett explained with a laugh. "He'll get busy playing arcade games with his friends and forget all about us."

He led her to a booth tucked far away from the blaring jukebox. The vinyl booths were a garish red, typical of a pizza joint, and Callie stuck to the seat as she slid toward the wall.

As a waitress approached, Rhett slid in next to her, sending Callie's heart slamming against her rib cage. Her equilibrium became even more off balance when he casually rested his right arm over the seat back.

"What can I get you to drink?" asked the waitress with a practiced smile, and Callie silently blessed her for giving her something else to think about besides Rhett's nearness.

"Cola," Rhett answered.

"That sounds good. I'll have one, too." Callie slid her glance to Rhett and smiled.

"Domestic bottles and beer on tap is two for one until six," the waitress suggested in a monotone, not looking as if she cared much one way or another. "Happy hour, you know?"

"Thank you, but no," Rhett said, friendly and polite, sending the waitress off with their two soda orders.

"What about Brandon?" Callie asked, amazed she could think straight, never mind find her voice, in this close a proximity to Rhett.

"He'll get his own soda. Root beer from the fountain. It's his favorite."

Rhett turned his attention to the menu, giving Callie the much needed opportunity to adjust to the curves being thrown at her.

Why was he sitting next to her?

She slid her glance to Rhett, but he appeared

to be studying the menu and didn't notice her perusal.

Of course he didn't sit across from you.

She carried on her internal conversation, trying to reason with her treacherous emotions.

He and Brandon couldn't share one side of a booth, and it would be awkward for Brandon to sit with a cop—especially one who'd brought him home from the station only weeks before.

That's all it was. Courtesy. Rhett was simply the nicest, kindest man she'd ever met.

But her heart refused to hear it, preferring a tune of its own, a song where Rhett and Callie rode off into the sunset on a strong, gallant steed.

And, of course, the obligatory happily-ever-after. What fantasy would be complete without it?

All this, and she hadn't read a fairy tale in years. Maybe getting jarred playing football *had* shaken up some of her childhood brain cells.

"Pepperoni okay?" Rhett asked, breaking her away from her thoughts.

"Mmm. Yes. Extra cheese."

"And no anchovies." He signaled to the waitress and placed their order.

When she was gone, Rhett chuckled and shook

his head. "You'll get a real kick out of watching Brandon when the pizza arrives."

"How's that?"

Rhett was a "hand talker," someone who couldn't speak a sentence without gesturing with his hands. And every time he gestured with his right hand, Callie very nearly jumped out of her skin, especially when his fingers brushed the sensitive area on the back of her neck.

"You just watch," Rhett continued, appearing not to notice the way the casual stroke of his fingers in her hair was affecting her. "Brandon has a pizza beacon. The moment the waitress shows up with the goods, he'll be slouching in his seat as if he'd been there all along. And stuffing pizza in his face at the speed of light."

Callie chuckled, ultra-aware of the movement of his fingers in her hair. If he kept it up, or worse, slid his arm down to her shoulder, she wasn't positive her lungs would remember to function.

As it was right now, she could barely breathe, and had to coach herself.

Breathe in. Breathe out.

She'd make a great Lamaze instructor some day, she thought wryly.

"You might want to be careful of your fingers

when you go to get a slice of pizza for yourself,'' he suggested, brushing her shoulder blade.

Her breath caught. If anyone needed to be careful with their fingers...

"Around food, I mean. Especially pizza," he continued, stroking her hair.

"Brandon turns into an animal, starts eating everything and anything. It's not a pretty sight."

"No, I expect not." Callie unwrapped her silverware from the napkin and twirled the spoon around her fingertips.

Did Rhett feel the tension crackling in the air between them, or was it all one-sided, a figment of her overactive imagination?

"Why haven't you ever remarried?" she blurted.

It wasn't exactly small talk, but then again, Callie had never been good at keeping her mouth shut when she should.

Rhett looked stunned, and Callie prayed for a hole to open up in the floor and swallow her.

Not only was her question serious and personal, but it was none of her business, and they both knew it. Blurting such a question out of the blue gave it the impact of a nuclear weapon detonating.

Chalk up a new most embarrassing moment for

Callie Brockman. But there was no sense dwelling on it. She couldn't take it back.

She sipped at her soda and plunged forward. "Let me guess. Your Desired Attributes in a Wife list is so lofty a real woman can't possibly hope to attain that status. Impossible to fulfill. So long it makes Santa's list seem like child's play."

Rhett took his time answering, thoughtfully tapping the menu against the table, turning it at square corners with every tap.

At long last, he smiled, which Callie took as a positive sign.

"Okay. I admit I had a list."

"You did?" He couldn't have surprised her more if he'd said he was already married.

He shrugged. "I didn't write it down," he protested. "But I guess I was looking for a certain type of woman. It was more of a mental list."

"Enlighten me," she begged, keeping the teasing tone in her voice. "We women have shared our list for centuries, but you guys have been a little tight-lipped."

"Yeah? I'm interested. What's this womanly list of manhunting? I married young, so I must have missed that information."

She winked at him. "Oh, come on. You

couldn't possibly have missed it. It's been around since Adam and Eve.''

"It has?'' Absently, he brushed the hair on her neck with his fingers, making it exceedingly hard for her to concentrate.

"Why, tall, dark and handsome, of course. Don't tell me you haven't heard that before.''

Rhett laughed. "You were beginning to have me worried. I thought maybe I really missed out.''

She gave him a blatant once-over. "Believe me, Rhett,'' she said, her voice husky, "you didn't miss out on one of them. Tall, dark and definitely handsome.''

He blushed. Thirty-some-odd years old, and he actually blushed! Callie was beginning to like this game.

"You're going to laugh if I tell you what I thought,'' he said, chuckling softly.

"Do tell.''

"I wanted a woman who baked homemade cookies.'' He was blushing again.

"I make homemade cookies,'' she blurted, then immediately regretted it. When was she ever going to learn to leave well enough alone and keep her *mouth shut?*

He grinned. "You certainly do. And I have to say, they were the best sugar cookies I've ever tasted."

Callie folded her hands on the table and stared through them. *Oh boy.*

They sat silently, each with their own thoughts, for several minutes, then Rhett turned to her, his free hand stroking her chin. "Truth?"

"Truth."

"I think God's got a wife already planned for me."

Normally, she would have laughed derisively at such a statement, but not with Rhett's green eyes, almost brown in the hue of his brown leather jacket, shining with his faith.

"How are you supposed to know she's the right one?" she asked, and realized she honestly wanted to know.

"I'll know," he affirmed resolutely. "Here." He thumped himself on the chest. "Faith is the substance of things hoped for, and the evidence of things not seen."

She assumed the quote was from the Bible, though she'd never heard it before. Rhett's words— or maybe more accurately, *God's* words—branded themselves in her mind.

"So she has to be a Christian," she said, as a statement rather than a question.

Rhett nodded. "God will work it out."

She reached up and ran the backs of her fingers across the rough stubble of his cheek. "I hope you find her. I really do."

Callie could hear the mental *scritch-scratch* of her name being crossed off Rhett Wheeler's list. And for some reason, that rejection hurt more than she thought it would, or should.

But she didn't blame Rhett.

His faith was important—no, *vital*—to his life. Callie couldn't share that, though she wished with all her heart she could.

"I'll know her when I see her." He sounded so sure of himself and of God, that Callie believed him. How could she not? God was real, for Rhett.

"Pizza," exclaimed Brandon, appearing just as miraculously as Rhett had said he would. Moments later, a huge, steaming pepperoni pizza with extra cheese was set on their table.

"You know, Brandon," said Rhett with a casual smile, "since we've been playing football this afternoon, it got me to thinking."

Brandon only nodded, as his mouth was already full of pepperoni pizza.

Rhett put his elbows on the table and steepled his fingers. "About football."

Callie's throat caught, as she realized where Rhett was directing the conversation. She remembered that first night they met, when she'd accused him of being a bad father.

That seemed so long ago, now. She hadn't known the tremendous integrity of the man beside her.

"Is it too late for you to go out for the Prospectors team?"

Brandon shook his head. "They're only halfway through training camp. Why?"

"So you can still walk on?"

"Sure." Brandon took another bite of pizza, nearly half a slice in one mouthful.

"Good. I'm glad to hear it. I want you to walk on. You deserve your shot at the varsity team. I'm only sorry I didn't tell you earlier, or that I ever said you couldn't go out for the game at all."

Brandon shook his head and took a long gulp of soda to wash down his pizza.

Callie raised her eyebrows at Brandon's denial. She glanced at Rhett to see how he was taking it, and saw a mirror image of her expression on his face.

"Why not?"

Brandon put his palms to his head and shoved his fingers through his hair. He looked more uncomfortable now than the night she'd brought him home from the police station.

"Talk to me, son," Rhett said, his voice low and even.

"I don't want to play football, Dad."

Rhett frowned, his dark eyebrows forming a *V* over his nose. "Come again?"

"I don't want to play football."

Rhett turned his gaze to Callie. "Do I have cotton in my ears, or did my son just say he didn't want to go out for football?"

"Sounded that way to me," she said lightly.

He turned back to Brandon. "Why don't you want to play football? You've always wanted to play football, ever since you were six years old. Of course you want to play football."

Rhett nodded and stuffed a breadstick in his mouth, saying without speaking that the subject was closed.

"You don't know what I want anymore," Brandon grumbled under his breath.

Callie had the sneaking suspicion the Wheeler men had just forgotten her existence. They glared at each other across the table, both too stubborn to speak.

Must be a family trait.

She decided to jump in, willing to risk her neck for the men in her life. "If you ask me, I think you should—"

Rhett and Brandon both jumped as if startled, then looked at her with a combination of surprise and annoyance.

She shrugged. "I just thought that...well, that you should talk."

Chapter Fifteen

"**We** *are* talking," Rhett said through gritted teeth. Naturally, a woman would have a different idea about what it meant to talk. But he was glad she was here with him, nonetheless.

Brandon scowled.

"Um, actually, no. You're ordering, and Brandon is growling. Pretty typical dad-teenager conversation, I think."

Now wasn't that just like a woman to point out the obvious, Rhett thought irritably.

He reached his arm around her and pulled her into the crook of his shoulder, brushing back her silky hair with his hand. He felt more confident when he had his arms around her. "You know what? You're right. I am being overbearing."

Brandon grinned.

"Don't agree," Rhett warned.

Brandon shrugged. "I didn't say anything."

"You didn't have to."

"Shall we start again?" Callie asked, a little too brightly.

"You should have been Ann Landers," Rhett grumbled, pulling her closer so she knew he was kidding.

He leaned forward, wanting to convey the intensity he felt. Brandon would never know how much Rhett loved him, but he could communicate some of what he felt.

"Talk, Brandon. I'm serious. I know I haven't paid enough attention to you. But I'll make you a promise. Right here, right now, I'm listening to you."

Brandon looked away for a moment, and Rhett wondered if it was his imagination, or if he saw the sheen of tears in his son's eyes.

Either way, Rhett swallowed hard.

"I like football," the boy admitted. "But that's not what I want to do with my life."

With Callie's encouragement, Rhett nodded.

"What I really want to do is be like you."

Callie reached across the table and took Brandon's hand. "You are like your father. More than you'll ever know."

The boulder in Rhett's throat grew larger, and he found it difficult to swallow.

"What I mean is, I want to work with you, Dad. I like what you do with the therapy dogs and stuff. I want to do that, too."

"My therapy dogs?" Rhett questioned, stunned.

He would never have suspected his son to be interested in social work—which just went to show how little he really knew about the boy he'd been living with for the past sixteen years.

Brandon's blue eyes lit with enthusiasm. "What you do with those dogs and those kids is just awesome, Dad."

Rhett grinned so wide he thought his face might split. His son wanted to follow in his footsteps. Who would have guessed? He certainly had no clue.

"That's why you stole that shirt, isn't it, Brandon?" Callie asked softly, and the question was like a knife in the chest for Rhett. "So you could be near your father, have some of the attention he gives to the delinquent kids he works with. And the dogs."

Brandon nodded for Callie's benefit, but his

gaze was locked on Rhett, who didn't know *what* to say. He did know what to do, though——kick himself in the backside a thousand times over for not realizing Brandon's desire earlier.

"I want to learn about your work. I want to help people like you do." His enthusiasm was contagious, and excitement brimmed from his eyes.

"Really?" Rhett hoped he didn't sound as choked up as he felt.

"I guess I pretty much have to participate in the therapy dog program, at this point," Brandon said, looking chagrined but pleased.

"Yeah, I guess you pretty much do," Rhett agreed. "I suppose you'll have to join ASAP."

He stopped and grinned. "How does Monday after school grab you?"

Callie reached under the table for his free hand and squeezed it hard, making his heart nearly stop. Her hand was so soft and warm, he was disappointed when she pulled it away.

"Can I go now?" Brandon asked, easily switching to an unrelated topic in typical teenage fashion.

"Get out of here," Rhett said affectionately.

When his son was out of hearing distance, he

turned to Callie, who was beaming at him, her eyes full of tears.

"Did I do something wrong?" he asked, concerned.

"No," she said, sniffling. She wiped her eyes with the corner of her napkin and flashed him a wavering smile. "You did everything right."

"Well, that's a first," he quipped. "Sometimes I feel like a real lughead."

"You're not."

"Glad to hear it." He balled up his napkin and tossed it on the table.

"So…" he said casually, though what he was feeling was anything *but* casual, "What are your plans for tomorrow morning?"

"Sunday? The usual. Sleep in. Clean house. Watch TV. Why do you ask?"

"A couple of reasons."

"And they are…?"

"First," he said, making an effort to catch her gaze and hold it, "I'd like you to attend church with Brandon and me."

Her eyes widened until she looked like a deer caught by headlights.

"If you aren't comfortable with that…"

"Oh, no. It's not that. It's just that no one has ever invited me to church before." She looked away, over his left shoulder, and her silver eyes glistened with tears.

"You've never been to church?"

"I went when I was a kid. But no, not as an adult. "Except that time with Brandon in the gym," she added with a shrug. "And I guess that doesn't really count, since I didn't actually make it to the service."

He brushed her cheek with his palm. "Then it's high time for you to go, don't you think?"

After a long pause, she spoke. "Yes. I do think." She grinned, putting him at ease. "What's number two?"

Rhett surreptitiously glanced around to make sure Brandon was out of hearing distance—not that he was overly concerned about it in a restaurant with the flashy lure of the brassy chirp and bang of video games.

"I want you to go with me to a breeder's kennel."

Her eyebrows rose in surprise. "I thought you got your dogs from the pound."

"I do." He paused and bowed his head toward her ear. "But this puppy isn't for the therapy dog program."

His heart welled in his chest and he grinned secretively. "At least, not directly."

Callie squealed and clapped her hands together. "Brandon!"

Rhett chuckled, feeling so happy he thought he might burst. "Yes, Brandon."

"What kind of dog are you getting him?"

As soon as she'd asked the question, she slapped a hand over her mouth and looked furtively around. "Oh, good. He's not around."

"If you really want to know," he said, trying to look as mysterious as possible, "I'll pick you up at 8:00 a.m. tomorrow morning."

"That's all you'll tell me?" she asked, laughing and playfully swatting him with her napkin.

"Oh, yeah. Don't you like surprises?"

"Of course. What woman doesn't?"

"Until tomorrow, then." Rhett popped another breadstick in his mouth, and the subject was closed.

For real this time.

Chapter Sixteen

Callie was pleasantly surprised to find she wasn't as uncomfortable at the church service as she'd imagined she'd be. The small community chapel was lovely, and the people were friendly, introducing themselves one after another and telling her how glad they were that she'd attended their service.

The oddest part about the service was the pastor's message. He presented a heartrending tale of God on a cross, forgiving those who crucified Him.

How could Jesus forgive the men who took his life?

She puzzled over that long after they'd gone on

to the holy Eucharist and the closing hymn. This was a Jesus she hadn't met before, and she tucked the church bulletin into her purse so she could look up the passage in the Bible later, when she was alone.

Rhett was bouncing around like a kid on Christmas morning, anxious to be underway.

"God's really watching out for me," he exclaimed as he opened the car door for her and then slid behind the wheel. He let out a low whistle that sounded almost more like a cheer.

Callie grinned at his enthusiasm.

"I just happened to know about these puppies, and the timing couldn't be better. They're eight weeks old and ready for a new home."

"Am I still supposed to be in the dark as far as this puppy goes?" she teased.

He chuckled. "Okay. I guess I can let the cat— or *dog,* to be precise—out of the bag."

She slapped him playfully on his arm. "Oh, Rhett. You're teasing me again."

"I like to see you blush."

She grinned. "You better watch yourself, big guy. I like to see you blush, too."

His eyebrows disappeared under his hairline. "Do you, now?"

Callie looked away, knowing that the blush

they were speaking of was spidering up her neck and onto her cheeks at that very moment.

When had it gotten so warm in here? She pulled on the collar of her blouse, wishing she'd thought to change into jeans and a T-shirt instead of the blouse and skirt she was wearing.

Panty hose weren't exactly an asset when going to look at a litter of puppies.

They pulled up to the breeder's house, an old-fashioned log-paneled A-frame, and as Callie stepped from the car, she immediately recognized that wasn't the only difference between this house nestled at the end of the block, and the others.

The backyard, a field, really, was deafeningly busy with the cheerful yip and bark of playful canines. Callie froze, her instinctive fear of dogs rising to the surface. Then she met Rhett's concerned gaze and found courage.

Rhett led her around the side of the house and through a chain-link gate to the back porch, where the breeder waited with nine roly-poly golden retriever puppies, ranging from a large, almost bronze-colored pup to a small, cream-colored fellow.

After Rhett introduced Callie to the breeder, a fifty-something lady named Tamara whose branding trait was her short, spike-tufted red hair, they were encouraged to interact with the pups—and their sire and dam, which were both on the property.

It was important to see the parents, Rhett explained, because that was a good indication of how the pups would turn out. These goldens were both of champion lineage, and had each earned titles in their own right.

Callie was amused by that fact, though she kept her thoughts to herself. While Rhett made a point of "rescuing" dogs from the pound for his therapy dog work, he wanted a certified, papered pup for his son.

Rhett reached for the bronze-colored girl, while Callie followed the cream-colored boy, who was, she decided after looking the other puppies over, the runt of the litter.

That probably explained why her heart went out to the little guy, whom she'd already mentally christened Butterboy. She had a perpetual weak spot for stragglers, especially one with the spunk and fight this little guy was showing.

Rhett pushed the bronze-colored puppy toward her, and she held the cuddly ball of fur in her arms, turning her on her back to scratch her tummy.

"What do you think of her?" Rhett asked, his

face beaming with enthusiasm. "She's the biggest one of the bunch. Tamara said she was born first. And she's very laid-back. She likes to be held and cuddled."

Callie nodded and put the puppy down on the ground to see what she'd do. She whined and scratched at Callie's leg to get back into the warmth of her embrace.

"I like her," Callie admitted, "but I have to say this little guy stole my heart from the moment I saw him." She pointed toward the cream-colored pup, who was pulling at his big sister's tail and growling playfully.

"Stole your heart, huh?" Rhett chuckled and scooped up the runt. "Maybe he could teach me a lesson or two."

Callie's breath caught in her throat when he winked at her, but she reminded herself he was only teasing her. Hadn't he told her just moments ago that he liked to see her blush?

"I don't know what it is about him, but something…I think Brandon will really like him. What do you think, Butterboy?"

Rhett raised an eyebrow. "Butterboy?"

"Well, I had to call him *something*."

"Yeah, but *Butterboy*?"

Callie laughed. "Hey, I was under pressure."

She reached out and scratched Butterboy behind the ears. He barked and wriggled, attempting to remove himself from Rhett's grasp and go back to Callie.

"Butterboy," Rhett said again, crossing his arms over his chest. "Hmm. Well, what I want to know is if you're going to come over and dog-sit when he starts barking and whining in the middle of the night? I'm pretty certain that dark puppy won't keep me up nights, but I don't know about this little guy here. He looks like a handful."

She sat down cross-legged and Butterboy immediately crawled into her lap and nipped at her fingers. She was glad he was playing—he had razor sharp teeth that hadn't been dulled by years of chewing.

Rhett crouched by her and offered his finger for dessert, laughing when Butterboy wrestled with his hand.

"You're the dog expert," she insisted. "You'd know better than I would which puppy is the best, especially to use in therapy dog work."

She chuckled when Butterboy jumped up on his hind legs and licked her chin. "Besides, it'll be Brandon's dog. You're definitely a better authority where your son is concerned."

Rhett grimaced. "I don't know about that."

She reached out and squeezed his hand, not knowing what to say, or how to talk her way out of it.

Rhett didn't react, except to scoop the puppy off her lap and turn him over in his hand, tickling his tummy. The puppy wiggled, but accepted the treatment with relative, if squirmy, equanimity.

After another minute of silent inspection, including taking a good look at Butterboy's teeth, Rhett turned to Tamara, who'd been sitting quietly on the porch, allowing them to interact with the puppies at their leisure.

"We'll take Butterball," he said, dropping the pup into Callie's lap while he fished for his wallet.

"But, Rhett—"

He cut her off, his eyes glinting with amusement. "I brought you for a reason. Picking a puppy is a heart thing. I knew you'd pick the one most suited for my son. And I was right. So don't argue."

Rhett grinned at the breeder and pointed at the cream-colored puppy again. "This one."

"But, Rhett…"

"I told you not to argue."

"I was just going to point out that Butterball is a turkey. It's Butter*boy* you're buying."

He laughed and shook his head. "Okay, but

I'm warning you—Brandon is *not* going to go for that name.''

She shrugged and tried to look offended. ''I didn't expect him to.''

After getting the papers signed and the pup in a carrier, they headed to Rhett's house to find Brandon.

''Have you talked to your brother yet?'' Rhett asked, thinking of how upset she'd been when Colin had arrived in John Day.

Callie looked away. ''No. I don't want to think about that today.''

He chuckled. ''Okay, Scarlett O'Hara.''

''Hey, it worked for her,'' she protested. ''Tomorrow *is* another day.''

''Has he tried to contact you?''

She frowned and shook her head. ''No. I thought he might, but he didn't.''

''I think he's giving you space to come to grips with his return.''

''Maybe.''

Rhett knew he was treading on thin ice, but he continued anyway. ''I think that shows how much he loves you.''

Her eyebrows scrunched so low he could hardly see her eyes. ''How's that?''

''If he didn't care so much, he would have

pushed you to accept him back in your life. Or at least called you a lot.''

Callie sighed. "Yeah. I guess you're right.''

"So when are you going to call him?'' he gently pressed.

"Talking about puppies was much nicer.''

"I know. But you can't put it off forever.'' He pulled his car to the curb and cut the engine. "You have to work this out eventually.''

Callie was out like a flash, opening the back seat door so she could get Butterboy's carrier. "I hope Brandon's home.''

Rhett nodded in agreement and let the subject drop.

Callie's situation was between her, Colin and God. He only hoped she considered him enough of a friend to turn to him if she needed help.

Besides, he was probably digging up old dirt on Callie just to keep from thinking of his own collection of problems. Brandon had said he wanted a dog, but Rhett worried nonetheless.

At least his son was home, if the regular pump of a bass guitar was any indication. What was it about teenagers that made them feel the need to turn their music high enough to break the sound barrier?

"You'd better go in and get that kid to turn his

music off," Callie suggested. "It'll scare poor Butterboy to death."

"Tell you what. You take B-boy out back, and I'll bring Brandon outside to meet him." He took a deep breath and brushed his fingers through his hair. "I hope he'll be surprised."

She rubbed her palm against his biceps, encouraging him even without the words that followed. "Don't worry, hon. He'll be surprised."

"Brandon Adam," he called up the stairs, trying to sound as if he were angry. "Get your sorry carcass down here."

The same words he'd used the night he met Callie. How appropriate.

"And turn off that music!"

Immediately the pounding bass ceased, much to Rhett's satisfaction. Had he ever been young?

"What's up?" Brandon asked, taking the stairs three at a time. His expression said, *What have I done now?*

"Get out here," Rhett demanded, pointing to the back door. "I can't believe you, boy."

Brandon frowned and headed out the door, Rhett moving in right behind him.

"I don't know what I di—"

He came to an abrupt halt in both word and action as his eyes lighted on the puppy.

Rhett grinned. "I thought this little fellow might come in handy in the therapy dog program."

Brandon whirled around, his whole face beaming. "It's for me?"

"*He's* for you," Callie corrected.

"Trust me. You *don't* want to know what she calls the poor fellow," Rhett added, enjoying the color that rose to Callie's cheeks.

"Brandon can name him," she insisted. "I just needed something to call him besides puppy, at least until we brought him home."

Brandon dropped to his knees and the golden retriever sprang for him. They tussled back and forth, the puppy yipping and the boy laughing.

"He's really mine," he said as if he needed to hear the words again to make them true. "To keep."

Laughing, Callie sat down on the lawn. "Come here, Butterboy," she called, slapping her thigh and making kissing noises.

"Butterboy?" Brandon protested.

"Well, his fur is the color of butter." She defended her choice of names with a dignified sniff.

"I told you that name wouldn't fly," Rhett teased. "It sounds like he's supposed to be for Thanksgiving dinner."

"Butterboy," Brandon said again. "Butterboy. Butter...*B*... Hey! How about Bullet? Here, Bullet, boy!"

The dog apparently liked his new name, for he made a beeline to Brandon.

Callie stood and stretched. "I like it. It fits his personality." She reached as if to pet the puppy, then ruffled Brandon's hair instead.

"Congratulations, kiddo," she said, affection lining her voice.

Rhett could only watch her, as he was both speechless and breathless.

What a difference a woman could make in this bachelor dad's life, never mind his son's. Callie was some special woman. He was beginning to think he might have to keep her.

Chapter Seventeen

Rhett felt foolish standing on Callie's doorstep and holding his breath like a teenager on his first date. He'd missed all this in high school, since he'd already been dating Kayla. Dating was an entirely new experience for him, and he wasn't sure he liked it. "Will you go to the homecoming dance with me?"

Understandably, her eyebrows disappeared under her hairline, but she recovered quickly. "Come again?"

Rhett cleared his throat and tried again. "I...er...wanted to know if you'd come with me to—"

"The homecoming dance. Yes, I heard that part."

"That's all I said."

Callie laughed. "I'm not sure I get it."

"What's to get?" Rhett parried, relaxing. As was typical whenever Callie was around, he felt at ease and completely, vibrantly alive and wonderful. "You, me, the dance..."

"Is this invitation in some official capacity? You need an extra cop on the premises to keep things under control?"

"In a small town?" He chuckled. "No, actually I—" he shifted from one foot to the other "—need a date. That is, if you're not busy."

She laid a hand on his arm. "I'd love to."

Grinning, he blew out the breath he hadn't realized he'd still been holding.

"When is the dance?"

He shrugged apologetically. "Tonight."

"Tonight?" she screeched.

"I know it's late notice..."

"Rhett, a *week* is late notice. This borders on *insanely* late. What time?"

"Er...now."

She nodded and pursed her lips. "Now, why am I not surprised?"

He dug into the pocket of his bomber jacket. "I bought you a corsage," he said, thrusting the orchid at her.

She took the flower graciously but didn't comment, which was a rare enough occurrence for Rhett to ask, "I haven't stunned you speechless, have I?"

A smile hovered on her lips, and as she raised her gaze, amusement brimmed from her sparkling eyes. "It's just that it's been a—ahem—a *while* since anyone's asked me to homecoming."

"Then you'll go?" He gave her his best wide-eyed puppy-dog look. "For me?"

"Well…" she hedged. "I'll miss the reruns of my favorite sitcom…."

"Please?"

"When you put it that way, how can I refuse?"

Her smile was contagious, and it left an imprint on Rhett's heart long after she'd run down the hall to change.

When she emerged from the hallway, the result was every bit as effective as if she'd waltzed down a grand spiral staircase. Rhett was the one stunned speechless. The short, sleek white dress subtly set off every womanly curve.

Rhett swallowed hard, and didn't stop gawking until she'd slid her arm through his.

"You're staring."

He cleared his throat. "Sorry."

"Is my dress not appropriate? Should I change

into something different? I didn't have much notice to prepare," she slid an accusatory glance at him, "so I grabbed the first dress I found."

"It's perfect," Rhett choked out.

"I feel self-conscious," she continued. "I don't wear a dress very often. Will I embarrass you?"

If it had been any other woman, Rhett would assume she was fishing for a compliment; but with Callie, she appeared genuinely distressed, and he scrambled to put her at ease.

"Embarrassed? I'm going to be the envy of every man there."

"Speaking of which, why exactly are we going to this dance? I'm assuming most of the *men* there will be a little young for me."

Rhett chuckled. "I forgot I'd promised to chaperon until Brandon came downstairs in a suit."

It took only minutes to drive to the school. Callie held back when they made their entrance, but Rhett urged her on. He hadn't been lying to suggest he was proud to have her on his arm.

Brandon spotted them nearly the moment they walked in, and shyly introduced his pretty, vivaciously giggly girlfriend Kim to Callie. Brandon neglected to mention Callie was his parole officer,

Rhett noticed; rather, she was introduced as Rhett's friend.

He was pleased to know that was true. As much as he treasured their working relationship, he much preferred the evenings at home they'd been spending together, sometimes talking late into the night, and sometimes splurging with popcorn and videos.

Giggling, Kim whispered something in Brandon's ear that made him grin, and the two teens slipped away. Rhett hardly noticed. In fact, very little caught his attention besides every gesture and nuance of Callie Brockman. Some moments he felt he could barely breathe, and other times he was light-headed, as if he'd taken in too much air.

Callie fidgeted, uncomfortable in her hose and heels, and even more disturbed by the odd way Rhett looked at her. She was wishing back the familiarity of true-blue polyester; anything to ward off this belated attack of adolescent awkwardness. She turned her thoughts to the music, but the pounding pulse of the bass coming from the speakers was enough to make her deaf for a week.

She breathed a sigh of relief when the DJ announced a slow set. But it was only a momentary blessing, for the DJ's next words shattered that moment of peace.

"I have a young man here who'd like to dedicate this song to his dad and his...parole officer?"

Callie's heart stopped dead as the DJ hooted with glee. "Now there's a combination for you. Dad and Cop, you know who you are."

The DJ put on a tango, at least Callie thought it was a tango, or maybe a mambo, well, something with a Latin beat, anyway.

Rhett dragged her halfway to the dance floor before she realized his intentions. "I can't dance," she whispered, pulling back with all her weight.

Rhett chuckled. "Well, I can. I'll lead."

It was *much* more complicated than that. Callie had the proverbial two left feet, and dance lessons as a young single hadn't helped her a bit.

"You didn't say I had to dance," she whispered frantically.

Rhett continued to look unfazed, and shrugged casually. "Well, they do call it a *dance* for a reason, you know. Besides, we'll hurt Brandon's feelings if we don't dance."

"Oh, well, I..." She was suddenly wishing for the loud, fast music she'd moments before been wishing away. Reluctantly, she allowed Rhett to lead her to the dance floor. "Don't say I didn't warn you," she muttered under her breath.

As he took her in his arms, his soft, clean scent enveloped her. She felt dizzy, and she wasn't sure whether it was nerves or Rhett's nearness.

"Hold on, sweetheart, 'cause we're gonna rumba," he whispered as he whisked her around.

She stumbled through the first few steps, but then the strong, syncopated music began to work its magic and she forgot about her feet, forgot about breathing. Her senses magnified until she could hear the beat of her own heart. As if in a dream, she forgot about everything except being in the arms of the man she loved.

Loved.

When the music ended and Rhett twirled her to a dip, her world turned upside down in more ways than one.

Chapter Eighteen

"Keep turning Bullet in a square," Rhett instructed, watching his son with the gangly puppy that, in a mere month, had learned how to sit, stay and heel to the boy's command.

"When can I start working with him off lead?" Brandon asked, keeping up with his exercise despite his obvious enthusiasm. "I think Bullet is ready."

"He may be, but you're not," Rhett said, laughing. "Learning to train dogs doesn't happen overnight."

Brandon commanded Bullet to sit, then let him off lead to run off his energy in the field house.

"Have you finished the book I gave you?"

"Yeah. But I'm going back through it, highlighting the areas I'll want to go back and study later."

"You're really serious about this, aren't you?" Rhett asked, pride welling in his chest. He'd never have thought his son would follow in his footsteps, yet Brandon had shown an amazing affinity, not only for dog training, but for working with people, as well. He didn't know how he'd missed his son's natural talent.

The boy didn't protest when Rhett insisted he clean kennels as an initiation into the business of social work and therapy dogs.

He spent his evenings reading dog-training books, saying he'd save his social work studies for college. And he'd been pestering Rhett for a week to take him on a *real* therapy dog visit.

"Tomorrow," he said aloud.

"Tomorrow, what?" asked Brandon, checking the food and water level of the dogs in the first two kennels.

"Tomorrow we'll go to Portland."

Brandon perked up. "For a therapy dog session?"

Rhett nodded, chuckling. "You have some community service to work off, remember?"

The boy had the good grace to look chagrined. "Yeah. Don't remind me."

"I'm going to invite Lance to come along, as well. He's almost finished his service, thanks to working with Bear."

Brandon caught his dad's gaze and held it, his look serious but his blue eyes gleaming with amusement. "Are you going to invite Callie?"

"Maybe. Why?"

"Because she's in love with you."

Rhett perked up as his heart took an emotional roller-coaster ride, but he tried to keep his expression in check. "What makes you say that?"

"Oh, come on, Dad. Everyone knows it."

"Define *everyone.*"

"At church. At the station. Everyone at school who saw you two dancing. Even Bobby the dispatcher thinks you guys should be married."

Rhett tried not to look *too* pleased. "He does, does he?"

Brandon nodded emphatically.

"Well, I guess the only important opinion in this situation is Callie's," he commented, wishing he felt as sure as his son looked.

"She's a goner, Dad, trust me on this. She's over here every day anyway. She might as well move in and save herself the trip. And you—"

"We weren't discussing me," he inserted hastily. "Do you think I should call her?"

Brandon rolled his eyes. "Dad!"

He looked as if he thought his father had lost all his marbles. Maybe he had, Rhett thought, reaching for the phone.

In any case, he'd lost his heart long ago to a silver-blond lady cop who annoyed him almost as much as she exhilarated him.

"Callie," he said when she answered.

Brandon waggled his eyebrows. Rhett narrowed his eyes on his son, then turned around and cupped the receiver for what little privacy that afforded.

"It's Rhett."

"Yes, I know," she said in a teasing tone.

"Was it something I said?" he quipped, and her laughter reverberated through the phone line.

"Brandon and I are going to Portland tomorrow for a therapy dog session at the hospital." He lowered his voice, though he knew Brandon was directly behind him, and was no doubt straining to hear his father make an idiot of himself over a woman. "I thought you might like to join us."

"I'd love to," she exclaimed, then fell into a sudden silence.

"Callie?"

"I can't go," she answered, sounding as if the words were forced from her throat. "I have... something else I have to do."

Rhett waved Brandon away and sat down at his desk, gripping the phone with both hands. "Does this something have to do with your brother?"

He could almost see Callie cringe at the question.

After another extended silence, she answered. "Yes."

"You're going to confront him."

"*Confront* isn't the word I'd use, but it's been a month and it looks like that stubborn, mule-headed brother of mine is taking up permanent residence at the Quest Motel."

"He still hasn't tried to contact you?" he asked, surprised.

He would have thought by now Colin would have either hunted her down and forced the issue, or given up on restoring the relationship and moved on to other things.

"No," she answered, sounding equally as surprised. "Not after that first time."

Rhett frowned, stroking the rough stubble on his chin with the curve of his pointer finger. He wanted to help, but how?

"Tell you what," he said at length. "How

about I take you out for breakfast tomorrow morning. Then we can go see your brother, and still have plenty of time to get to Portland with the dogs.''

"You'd do that for me?" She sounded choked up, but relief was evident in her voice.

"Of course," he agreed immediately, grinning despite the fact she couldn't see him. "Why should you have to face this alone?"

And that wasn't all. He had the sneaking suspicion this confrontation, or encounter, or whatever Callie wanted to call it, would make or break the relationship, not only with her brother, but with him as well.

It was time for his love for her to stand the test of family—sometimes the toughest test in a relationship.

He was still unclear about Callie's faith commitment, but she'd been attending church regularly, and had even mentioned one day that she'd been reading the Bible he bought her.

So they stood a chance. Maybe.

And it was that big *if* that loomed before them, feeling every bit as large as the Grand Canyon. They were being tested through fire—and Rhett wasn't positive he'd come out unscathed.

But he had to risk it. He just had to.

* * *

Callie turned up the radio, hoping the familiar tune would erase the fear and uncertainty from her mind.

She'd been avoiding the unavoidable, prolonging the inevitable. And yet...

This last month had seen a change in her. Spending time with Rhett and Brandon became the highlight of her day, and even when she wasn't with them, they were never far from her mind.

They almost felt like a *family*.

But she'd blown it with her own, so how could she hope to make it with Rhett and Brandon, who'd already been through so much?

The closer she became to the Wheeler men, the more she knew she needed to finish what Colin had started—to make right that which once was wrong. To 'fess up to her part in Colin's painful past, and try to make a new go of it, brother and sister—and even her father, though God would have to work that part out, since her father had died several years ago in a freak car accident.

She knew in her heart the time had come to make things right.

And the oddest part was, she felt ready, and it

was in part due to Colin's words on the day he'd returned.

She'd been thinking over that vacation Bible school experience, remembering the sanctity of the moment when she gave her heart to Jesus.

Was that just a childhood thing, or did it really mean something eternal?

Until she answered that question, she couldn't commit to Rhett, and she knew the relationship between the two of them was deepening to the point where commitment—*permanent* commitment—was more than a possibility. More like a probability.

She loved Rhett and Brandon with her whole heart, but they were both committed to the Lord. That stood between them like a chasm, and neither she nor Rhett could bridge that gap.

It had to be God.

Somehow, some way, the God whom she'd once denied even existed had to bring her over to His side of the playing field. And how He would do that, Callie couldn't say. She only knew she had to see Colin again, and take what came afterward one baby step at a time.

So when Rhett picked her up for breakfast, she was shaking with nerves, feeling as if her whole existence pivoted on this one point in time.

"Nervous?" Rhett asked in the car on the way to the Quest Motel.

She tittered through a scratchy throat. "Do I look it?"

He glanced at her and grinned. "Yeah."

"It figures. Where's the cop persona when I need it?"

"I don't think you need it, sweetheart," he said softly. "Just be yourself. And don't be shocked if Colin surprises you."

Five minutes later, she was standing before the door to Colin's room, trying to force air into her lungs when they refused to work on their own. She was feeling a little woozy, and wanted to sit down.

"You're hyperventilating," Rhett commented as he placed a reassuring hand on her back.

"I don't suppose you have a paper bag handy," she joked, though in truth she was quivering with apprehension.

"Don't take deep breaths, just slow ones," he counseled, pulling her to him for a hug. "And don't forget I'm right by your side."

"How could I forget?" She laughed shakily. "You're all that's holding me up."

"Are you going to be okay?"

She nodded. "I'm sure I'm making more out

of this than it really is. Colin is my twin, after all."

She reached her hand up to knock and jumped back when the door flew open before she could lay a hand on it.

"Callie!" Colin exclaimed as surprise turned to pleasure.

He enveloped Callie in a bear hug, which by necessity included Rhett, also, since his arm was still firmly around her waist.

"Colin Brockman," he said, stepping back and thrusting out his right hand. "Callie's twin."

"Rhett Wheeler," he said without hesitating. "Callie's told me a lot about you."

Colin's glance went from Rhett to Callie, and then back to Rhett again. "Good stuff, I hope."

"What else?" inserted Callie, wanting to keep control of the conversation. "Rhett is with social services, so we work together," she said by way of explanation.

Colin gestured them both inside. "Any friend of Callie's is a friend of mine," he said, the humorous sparkle in his sky-blue eyes, remarkably like Callie's, indicating he suspected the relationship between his sister and the social worker was more than just friendship.

"Were you going out?" Callie asked, parking

herself on one of the two double beds. "We can come back later."

Rhett's gaze flashed to hers, telling her without speaking that they were going to take care of this now, one way or the other.

"I was just going for a walk in the park. I've had a lot of time alone to think."

Callie looked down at her shoes. "I'm sorry about that," she said through a dry throat. "I should have come earlier."

Colin held up his hands. "No. I realized after I'd already contacted you that barreling into your life wasn't exactly the most brilliant way of re-establishing our relationship."

"It's my fault, too, Colin. I won't let you take all the blame."

"Let's call it even, then," he suggested with a wide smile.

"Now," he said, sitting on the bed across from Callie and rubbing his palms together, "did you bring a social worker to counsel us through this?"

Rhett chuckled and waved them away. "I'm only here for moral support."

"And physical support. I was so nervous before I came in here I nearly lost my footing."

"I'm glad someone is looking out for my sis," Colin said, flashing Rhett a grateful smile.

"Oh, believe me, she's the one looking out for me," Rhett said. "I'd be happy to pay her back just a little for all she's done for my son and me."

"He's exaggerating," Callie said, chuckling.

Still, her heart beat double-time, seeing the way her twin and the man she loved sized each other up. There'd been a time when Colin was ready to take off the head of any guy stupid enough to ask his sister out on a date.

But that had been a long time ago. They weren't kids anymore. And what she felt for Rhett wasn't a teenage crush.

Colin's eyes shone with mirth as he watched his sister's expression. "This sounds like a story I'd like to hear sometime."

His smile faded, and he reached across the beds and took both Callie's hands in his. "But first, I'd like to know why you've come."

Callie's heart swelled up with so much love she wasn't sure she could contain it. She wanted to laugh and cry all at once.

The speech she'd planned—the one where she explained how God had touched her life, and how she now understood why Colin had come—went whistling out of her brain, leaving a big blank spot and a mountain of emotion in its place.

"I love you," she blurted, hurling herself into

her twin's arms. She *was* laughing and crying at the same time.

Then she found herself wrapped in two very strong sets of arms, one man on either side of her. "I love you," she said again, this time including Rhett in her proclamation. "And I'm making a royal fool of myself."

She sat back down on the bed and wiped her eyes while the men looked on. "I should have come to your graduation," she said to Colin. "And you'll never know how sorry I am that I didn't."

"I don't blame you for that, Callie. I know how Dad was. You didn't have a choice."

He paused and looked out the window. "I just wish we could talk to Dad now. Unresolved issues, and all that."

He was obviously trying for a light tone, but Callie could hear the pain in his voice.

"We can't change what's past," she said, wondering where this wisdom was coming from, "but we can forge on from here."

"Philippians," Colin said, hugging Callie one more time.

Yes, that was where she'd heard it before. "Listen to me, spouting Scripture. Go figure."

Both men beamed at her.

"God had this all planned out," Colin said, his assurance evident in his tone. "I would have had to leave tomorrow, whether you'd come to see me or not."

"Leave?" Callie repeated, aghast. "But we've only just started mending our relationship."

Rhett sat down next to her, and the comfort of his arm around her waist gave her the encouragement and strength she needed to deal with the new curve thrown at her.

"I'd love to stay, Callie, but I'm starting school on Monday."

"School? I thought you were in the navy."

Rhett ran his hand up and down her spine, and she focused on the movement instead of her flighty emotions.

"I am. I've managed to acquire my bachelor's degree there. But now—" he paused and licked his lips "—I'm going into the seminary, Callie. I'm going to be a navy chaplain."

"Oh, how wonderful!" Callie exclaimed, and realized only afterward that it was true. She *was* happy for her brother.

"I wish you the best," Rhett said, reaching out to shake Colin's hand.

"I'll be coming up here on breaks, so we can

get to know each other again. And we can spend the Christmas holiday together.''

He glanced from Callie to Rhett, then grinned. ''Maybe we'll have something else to celebrate?''

Callie's face felt as if she'd been baked in the sunshine, but Rhett only smiled.

''Maybe,'' he agreed, tightening his grip on Callie.

Now what, thought Callie, was *that* supposed to mean?

She could only hope.

Chapter Nineteen

Rhett checked the leashes on all the dogs, tightened the bright-red sashes that proclaimed them therapy dogs, then pronounced everyone ready to enter the hospital.

He'd decided not to bring a dog for himself so he could concentrate on the others, especially since he was bringing in three rookie people and one rookie dog.

Not that he anticipated trouble. He didn't. In fact, he couldn't think of more pleasant company than his son, the woman he loved and a kid who'd gone from belligerent to buoyant. He surveyed his team with a smile.

Brandon and Bullet both looked antsy and

wired. Callie, brimming with excitement, had her hands full with her black lab Merlin, who was at that gangly teenage-dog phase where everything he did looked awkward, and who was picking up on Callie's mood, which only made things worse for her. Lance stood nervously to the side, stroking Bear's head. Bear, of course, was just as laid-back as ever, ready and eager to party.

"They're waiting for us in the pediatric cancer ward, but just in case anyone else stops us and inquires about the dogs, let me do the talking," he instructed. "Usually, the therapy dog sashes are all we need to get through without a problem, but occasionally there's an overzealous janitor or something who thinks our dogs have germs."

His "crew" laughed nervously, and followed closely as he led the way into the hospital. No one stopped them, and they made their way to the children's cancer ward without incident.

Just before they entered, he pulled Callie aside, sliding his arm around her waist and pulling her close under his arm, just because he liked the feel of her there.

"I wanted to prepare you for what you'll see in there," he whispered for her ears only. "These kids look really sick sometimes, and many of them have lost their hair."

He smiled and squeezed her waist. "But they're God's children, and most of them are the toughest fighters you'll ever see in your life."

Callie set her jaw. "I'm ready. I won't make a scene."

Rhett chuckled. "I didn't think you would. But I know you have a heart of gold underneath that *tough cop* exterior, and I'd like to keep it that way."

He chucked her under the chin and gestured to the door, ready for his crew to do their work.

Callie—and Brandon and Lance, too, for that matter—looked like old pros at this job. Each of them moved between the beds, taking time to speak to each of the children personally, and allowing the dogs to do their good work, as well.

Even Lance, who Rhett admitted only to himself he'd been worried about, looked enthralled with the children, and happy to be helping out.

An hour passed in the blink of an eye, and the head nurse signaled casually for their departure from the ward. Rhett, in turn, waved his crew out, and led the way down the hall.

It wasn't until they'd hit the elevator that Callie broke down and cried silently, tears pouring down her cheeks, though she kept her thoughts to herself.

Rhett was so deep in thought, and Callie was crying so softly, he probably wouldn't have noticed, except that Brandon none too lightly nudged him in the ribs with his elbow and flipped his chin in Callie's direction.

Rhett reached for her and pulled her aside. "God gives meaning even to the shortest life," he said gently, but that only served to make things worse.

"I know," she said, pulling a tissue from her purse. "They were just so dear—and so brave. Their faith in God is astounding! I just feel blessed to have that small moment in time with them."

Rhett had been afraid of Callie's heart being broken. It was only now that he realized it was his own heart in the most jeopardy, seeing how the children in the cancer ward had affected his beloved Callie.

"I'm sorry," he said softly, wondering if he'd made a mistake to bring her here.

She looked up to him, misty-eyed. "When can we go back?"

Rhett's heart did a double whammy. Now why hadn't he expected that of her? She didn't pretend to be something she wasn't.

Callie Brockman was a strong, capable woman

who was able to see the bad in a situation yet work for the good with all her might.

How had he ever gotten by without her in his life?

Brandon nudged him again. "I think you guys should talk," he whispered.

Who was the adult here? Rhett wanted to snap, but Brandon only grinned and reached to take Merlin from Callie.

"You guys ought to visit the maternity ward before you go," his precocious son announced. "I'm sure Callie will feel better after she's seen a few babies."

"Brandon!" Rhett muttered, low and threatening.

Callie blew her nose. "You know, I think he's right. I would like to visit the nursery. There's always hope, isn't there? Even in the midst of death, there is life."

Rhett nodded to Callie, not knowing what to say to her profound philosophical revelation.

Instead, he turned back to his son, whom he did have words for. "You're getting away with it this time," he warned, "but don't think you're off the hook for good."

"Take your time," was Brandon's response. "Lance and I will handle the dogs just fine."

"Yeah," Rhett answered dryly. "I'm sure you will."

The elevator stopped on the first floor and the two boys, Brandon with his two puppies and Lance with Bear, exited ahead of Rhett and Callie, who had to go back up to the third floor if they were to visit the nursery in the maternity ward.

Rhett caught the door before it closed and kept it open with his palm. "Hey, Lance?"

Lance turned around, quite a feat in his baggy jeans, Rhett thought, and flipped his hair out of his eyes with a toss of his chin.

"Fine job today, son."

"Thanks, Mr. Wheeler," Lance answered, shuffling his feet and looking away. He was clearly not used to receiving praise from anyone, most especially adults.

"I want you to have Bear," he said, though he didn't know where the thought had come from. Now that he'd said it, though, he realized the strength of that idea, just how right it was.

"Me?" Lance sounded astounded.

"If your mom won't let you keep him at home, you're welcome to use the kennel at the field house for as long as you need it. But he's all yours, buddy."

"Why?"

It wasn't a belligerent question, but rather an astonished one. Lance looked as if he'd misheard, as if it couldn't be true. Excitement and apprehension boiled just under the surface, Rhett thought, watching the myriad of emotions cross the boy's face.

He reached out his free arm and clasped the boy's shoulder. "You've proven yourself responsible," he answered unreservedly. "And what's more, Bear has kind of gotten used to you. I don't think he'd like it much if another kid came along and tried to take your place."

Lance dashed his arm across the corners of his eyes and turned away, but Rhett could still hear what he said. "Thanks, Mr. Wheeler. I'll take good care of him. I swear I will."

Rhett, feeling kind of choked up himself, didn't know how to answer, so he let the elevator door close and punched the button for the third floor.

He felt as big and gangly as a teenager, with all this emotion floating around. He'd never been that affected by it before—social work had given him a hard heart, in some ways.

He wasn't sure whether or not this was a good time to regain what he'd lost, though. How would he ever get through these last few minutes with Callie?

He shifted his glance in her direction as nonchalantly as possible. She was crying again, and this time, she didn't bother to wipe the tears away.

Callie was wondering what she could possibly say to a man who'd just made a juvenile delinquent into a good citizen.

But words didn't seem enough to convey what she felt, so she remained silent.

She was more than a little embarrassed at Brandon's obvious attempts at matchmaking, but she couldn't see a way to gracefully bow out without hurting anyone's feelings, so she followed Rhett onto the third floor.

Unlike the cancer ward, the nurses here looked relaxed and smiling. This was a happy place to be.

One expectant mother trotted by her at a near jog, then stopped to grasp the handle attached to the wall when a contraction hit.

Callie's eyes widened, whether from the innate fear of childbirth, or from the lady's odd combination of actions, she couldn't say.

But the pregnant woman in question appeared to notice Callie's expression amidst all the puffing and blowing, and when her contraction was done, she high-stepped it back to where Callie and Rhett stood.

"Oh, you two must be checking out the ward. This is an excellent hospital. They have twelve birthing rooms, each with a theme. If you get here when it's not too busy, they even let you pick out the wallpaper." She stopped to pant and laugh. "When is your baby due?"

Callie blanched and Rhett cleared his throat.

"I'm not...that is... Why are you jogging down the hallway?" she asked instead.

Her diversionary tactic appeared to work, at least for the moment, and Callie breathed a sigh of relief.

"Helping the contractions along," the woman replied cheerfully. "My name is Janet, by the way."

She patted Rhett on the shoulder. "You two will learn all about labor and delivery in your Lamaze class."

She swept her hand toward Callie. "Enjoy it, honey. It's one of the few times in a woman's life where she gets her feet rubbed without begging for it. Mmm. Mmm. Mmm."

Callie wondered what rubbing a woman's feet had to do with having a baby, but she wasn't about to ask.

"We'll learn about it in Lamaze," Rhett echoed, sounding as stymied as Callie felt.

"Oh, yes. And all the panting and puffing, too. You get to be the coach, Daddy," she added, addressing Rhett.

"Okay," he answered hesitantly. "If you say so."

Callie wondered if Rhett had been present at Brandon's birth, but from the look on his face, she didn't think so.

That thought brought a smile to her lips, and the pregnant woman smiled back, though her forehead was glossy with a sheen of sweat.

"You don't get a ref's whistle or anything," Janet teased Rhett. "But you can wear a baseball cap if you want to."

He snapped his fingers. "And I had my catcher's mitt all ready to go."

The lady laughed, then groaned when another contraction hit.

Rhett moved to her side, supporting her by the arm that wasn't clamped white-knuckled to the handle on the wall. "Should I call a nurse?"

The woman held up a finger for him to wait, then panted her way through the contraction. "I don't need a nurse, honey, but I'd best be getting back to my room."

She took a deep breath and wiped off a drop of sweat that was threatening to drip off the tip of her nose. "This run-walk stuff appears to be working. That was only three minutes between contractions."

Callie thought she looked both excited and nervous, but then, who could blame her for either emotion, given the circumstances?

"My husband better get back up here pronto," Janet continued. "He went out for a burger. Wouldn't it just figure if he missed Jimmy's birth?"

"Jimmy?" asked Rhett, sounding confused.

"This is our third. We know it's a boy. He's been Jimmy since our five-month ultrasound."

"I didn't know you could do that," Callie exclaimed in wonder. "Know the sex of your baby, I mean."

"It's not an exact science, by any means—at least not with an ultrasound. But sometimes they can tell." Janet chuckled pleasantly.

"I think I'd rather be surprised," said Rhett, and Callie immediately turned her gaze on him, wondering if he was teasing.

He'd never looked more serious in his life.

He insisted on walking Janet back to her room, which Callie thought was terribly gallant, then obtained directions to the newborn nursery from Janet's husband, who had just arrived, and whose chin was smeared with mustard.

Callie restrained a laugh. The man really must have hurried with his meal.

Callie had been in a hospital once in her life— the day she was born. It made her nervous, and she wondered if she was taking on nervous energy from the maternity floor itself.

Labor and delivery. A baby of her own.

It wasn't something she'd given much thought to in the past. Until Rhett came along, she hadn't given *any* relationship much thought.

But now, staring at a row full of newborns behind warped Plexiglas, her opinions on relationships and babies did a sharp one-eighty.

"I'd like to have a baby of my own someday," she murmured, watching a newborn baby girl trying unsuccessfully to put her thumb in her mouth.

Unfortunately for the newborn, her fist kept getting in the way, and Callie laughed.

Rhett wrapped his arms around her waist and nestled his lips into the soft space at the back of her neck, sending shivers up her spine.

She froze, wanting to etch this moment in her memory. Right this instant, she was perfectly happy, perfectly content, and all was well with God and the world.

"You can have my baby," Rhett said, his voice low and husky.

She whirled on him, the spell broken. "I can't believe you said that!" she whispered harshly, not wanting to make a scene.

"What?" he responded, looking thoroughly flabbergasted. And annoyingly innocent. "What did I say?"

"You said... You said..."

She couldn't make herself say the words.

Rhett burst into laughter, gaining himself a stern look from the head nurse across the way. Callie tried to wiggle from his grasp as he reached his arms around her, but there was no stopping him from what he wanted, and it appeared, at the moment, that he wanted to hang on to Callie.

There was no doubt he could overbear her physically, so she simply froze in his arms and hoped her icy gaze would be enough to deter any *other* wandering thoughts that might be running through that mind of his.

He ignored her scowl and cocked his head until his forehead was touching hers and his warm breath caressed her cheek. "I wasn't coming on to you, Callie," he said with a chuckle, in that honey-rich voice that always made her knees turn to jelly.

Until *now*.

"I don't think this is anything to laugh about," she retorted. "And yes, you *were* coming on to me. I know a line when I hear it."

Again, he chuckled. "What I was trying to say—and what, I'm sure, Brandon is pacing around the car *hoping* I'll say, given his tactless hints—is, would you be my wife?"

Callie had been waiting her whole life for those words, but when she heard them, she couldn't believe they were true. "But you said..."

"That I'd like to have a baby with you." He grinned like the Cheshire cat. "And that's the God's honest truth. I want us to get married as soon as possible."

"As soon as possible?" she repeated numbly, waiting for her heart to start beating again.

"Tomorrow would be good."

"Tomorrow?" She screeched in full this time, and the head nurse sent another warning glare their direction.

"So Colin can be there. I'd hate for him to miss giving you away, and I surely can't wait for Christmas vacation to make you my wife."

"Your wife," she repeated, beginning to feel like a parrot, unable to come up with a thought or a word of her own, as every joyful emotion in the world washed over her in waves.

Callie couldn't think of a thing to say, but Rhett didn't seem to notice.

Apparently, he was lost in his own thoughts.

"My wife," he agreed enthusiastically.

He flashed her that heart-stopping, lopsided smile that made the laugh lines fan attractively around his warm green eyes, which were twinkling with merriment.

"And now," he said, kissing her between each word for emphasis, "maybe we can talk about those babies I mentioned...."

Epilogue

The young man set his jaw, his throat corded with strain. Surprisingly dark eyebrows scrunched grimly over wide blue eyes, a shady contrast to his closely cropped golden-blond hair. Long, muscular arms with hands tightly fisted crossed over a chest just beginning to show a hint of breadth.

He looked scared, completely out of his wits.

Callie smiled weakly and flashed a glance to the boy's erstwhile father. "Will you please explain to our son that babies have been coming for ages? He looks like he's about to have a nervous breakdown."

Rhett chuckled. He looked every bit as ruffled as Brandon: haggard from lack of sleep, his hair in adorable disarray. The Wheeler men. *Her* men.

"Callie did the hard part," he said, his voice gruff with emotion.

Callie waved him away. "Not that anyone can tell, what with you strutting around like a peacock," she teased affectionately.

Turning her attention back to her stepson, she asked, "Would you like to hold her?"

Brandon's gaze sprang to hers. "Me? Well, yeah. If you think I won't hurt her or anything."

"Piece of cake, kiddo," she assured him. "Your new sister is as excited to meet you as you are to see her." Callie carefully unwrapped the small bundle at her side. "Just support her neck to keep her head from bobbing."

Brandon didn't look too confident, and Rhett cavalierly moved to his side. "Hello, little pumpkinhead," Rhett crooned over the baby in a high, singsong voice.

"Please tell me you aren't going to call her that," Callie groaned.

"What's wrong with pumpkinhead?" He protested, looking offended.

"Her name is Abigail."

"Oh, but it's okay for you to name your truck Buck, and Brandon's dog—"

"Butterboy—I mean, *Bullet*—isn't the issue here," she interjected.

Abby squealed her agreement, and the three of them laughed.

Brandon held out a finger and laughed when the baby gripped it in her fist. The sight of her two favorite men with the precious gift of their new baby was almost too much happiness for Callie to bear. Her heart swelled until she thought it might burst. She silently thanked God for answering her prayers, even when she hadn't known she was praying.

Who knew that there could ever be such Love in the world?

*   *   *   *   *

Dear Reader,

Spending time in John Day, Oregon, with my characters in this novel, Rhett and Callie, was a special experience for me. Many of my extended relatives live in the John Day Valley, so it was a joy to bring to life a place where I spent many happy hours during my childhood.

But even more remarkable was the spiritual journey I experienced with these characters, from bitterness and resentment into joy and forgiveness.

As Callie Brockman learned, forgiveness is a choice, not an emotion. There's no mistaking that it's a tough choice to make, but usually the one we hurt most by clinging to the root of bitterness is us.

Jesus Christ forgave our sins when we were yet enemies of the cross. Can we in good faith do any less for those who've hurt or betrayed us?

I hope you'll take this moment to thank God for His wonderful gift of forgiveness, and to shed whatever burdens you may be carrying, as well; for His yoke is easy and His burden is light.

Your continued servant in Christ,

Deb Kastner

Love Inspired®

Heartwarming Inspirational Romance

Here's your opportunity
to sample another work by

Deb Kastner

#0-373-87096-5 **Black Hills Bride** $4.50 U.S.☐ $5.25 CAN.☐

(limited quantities available)

TOTAL AMOUNT	$
POSTAGE & HANDLING	$
($1.00 for one book, 50¢ for each additional)	
APPLICABLE TAXES*	$ _____
TOTAL PAYABLE	$ _____
(check or money order—please do not send cash)	